HIGH PRAISE FOR KATIE MAXWELL!

THE YEAR MY LIFE WENT DOWN THE LOO

"*The Year My Life Went Down the Loo* is a treat! Laugh-out-loud funny, full of sly wit and humor, poignant, realistic teenage angst, and expertly drawn characters, the book is impossible to put down."

—*Romance Reviews Today*

"Gripping, smart-alecky, shocking . . . and at the same time tender. A brilliant debut by Katie Maxwell!"

—*KLIATT*

"Fans of *The Princess Diaries* and other well written teen books will cheer this new entry to the scene."

—*Huntress Reviews*

"Girls of all ages will find themselves laughing out loud at Emily's crazy antics and experiences. . . . A great start to a great new series."

—Erica Soroco, teen correspondent for the *Press Enterprise*

"This debut book for Dorchester's new YA imprint is, in a word, refreshing. It's so true to life, dealing with an average teenage girl's issues instead of the mild and bland subjects covered in many other YA novels. Girls will laugh, sigh and squeal aloud as they embark upon Emily's journey."

—*RT BOOKClub*

THEY WEAR WHAT UNDER THEIR KILTS?

"A c̶̶̶̶̶̶̶̶̶̶̶̶̶̶̶

—*RT BOOKClub*

Reasons My E-mails From France Are Better Than a Fresh Croissant

1. Croissants make your butt huge, but my e-mails are non-fat and filled with very cool French slang that will make everyone think you're *avoir du chien* (that's French for "having dog"—it means you're très coolio!).

2. You learn about stuff croissants won't tell you (ha!), like how to karaoke in Paris, where to pee in Notre Dame when everything is closed, and what it's like to skate on possessed rollerblades.

3. Croissants go stale in a few days, but my e-mails are always up-to-date with the latest news on my überly-fabu boyfriend Devon and his snogalicious lips.

4. A croissant is tasty, but not as much fun as reading about my anti-teen-pregnancy baby doll Jack, and how he ended up with a blue mouth . . . and losing an arm, and an eye, and of course, there's the

Other *Smooch* books by Katie Maxwell:

THE YEAR MY LIFE WENT DOWN THE LOO
THEY WEAR *WHAT* UNDER THEIR KILTS?

What's French For "EW!"?

KATIE MAXWELL

SMOOCH NEW YORK CITY

SMOOCH ®

May 2004

Published by

Dorchester Publishing Co., Inc.
200 Madison Avenue
New York, NY 10016

ISBN 0-8439-5297-0

Printed in the United States of America.

Visit us on the web at www.smoochya.com.

What's French For "EW!"?

Subject: Guess what? I'm going to have a baby!
From: Em-the-enforcer@englandrocks.com
To: Dru@seattlegrrl.com
Date: 4 April 2004 9:19 pm

Did you freak? Heh heh heh.

Hola, chica, we're back from our trip to London! Oh, wait, I'm supposed to be getting ready for Paris. *Bonjour*, chicklette. *Nous returnez-vous* from Londonez. Or something like that. You know, if I weren't getting to spend two whole glorious parent-free weeks in Paris—city of loooooooooove—I would just give up trying this whole French thing, because it's majorly diffy! The grammar and stuff you have to learn! Sheesh! Like I have time?

Anyhoodles, when I got back from London, Holly called

and said she heard from Chloe T (you remember her—she's from Pennsylvania and has braces) that we're getting our babies this week. Chloe T's dad works for the company that makes the software they use in the babies, so she should know.

"Very cool and about time," I told Holly, putting some Wanton Woman Red polish on my toenails. "I hope I get a girl. Because, you know, dealing with a baby widdle-stick is just going to be too embarrassing. OHMIGOD! I just had a horrible thought! What if the baby is like a real one? What if it can pee on you? My friend Dru's cousin had a baby boy, and we were playing with it, and when Sara went to change it, it peed all over the front of her!"

"According to the pamphlet Miss Naylor gave us, they don't really pee, they just kind of excrete the water they suck in from the baby bottle," Holly said. "Chloe T says the reason they were delayed getting the babies to us is because they were upgrading the software, so now we'll have LuvMyBaby v4.75, which has the advanced behavior card, and a bigger memory chip so the babies can be used for up to a month without having to be taken in to have the care data downloaded."

"Ew. Who'd want a baby for a month? A couple of days is just fine with me. Short enough to be fun, and then it's bye-bye to pretend motherhood and hello to us in Paris having oodles of fun with Devon."

"I don't think I'd mind having one for a month if it was a nice baby," Holly said, sounding thoughtful. She's been doing a lot of that lately. It's kind of worrying me, to tell the truth. It's like she's become that woman in the opera your mom made us see last year—you know, the one where the woman had TB and was coughing up blood and guts and stuff, and was dying a lonely, tragic death. *Camille,* that's the name of it. Holly has been *Camille*-ing lately, acting very tragic and depressed, like she's suffering from something really bad. "I think it sounds like a very interesting experiment, although Mum says if she'd had a LuvMyBaby when she was going to school, she never would have married Dad and had us. Whatever sex baby I get, I just hope I don't get a colicky one. Chloe T said some of the babies are programmed to be fussy. I can't deal with a fussy baby, not when I'm going to go to Scotland for the weekend. You know how I break out if I don't get lots of sleep, and what will Ruaraidh think if I show up all spotty with big black bags under my eyes?"

"I'm telling you, apricot scrub is your best friend." I eyed my Wanton Women Red toes and decided another coat was needed. You know my toenail polish motto: two coats is good, but four is better. "Brother told me he read up on the 'show teens the horror of becoming a parent' program, and found out that the LuvMyBaby people set the babies to be really cranky so you never, ever want to have sex. I think that's cheating. I mean, some babies have to be good, don't you think? Mom says I hardly ever cried. Course, she thought I was mental or something because I didn't talk for a long time, but still, I was a good baby. So I don't buy all this hype they're feeding us about the babies being ultrarealistic and stuff if they're just really safe-sex propaganda."

"What do you think I should wear when I go to Scotland?" Holly asked, totally ignoring what I was saying, only in a nice way. I didn't really mind—even though she *is* getting to leave school early to go—because she wasn't sounding *Camille*-ish when she talked Scotland. I have to stay through the end of the semester because I missed that week last month when I had the flu so bad that I puked my guts up every time I got out of bed. Life is *so* unfair.

"Em? Are you still there?"

"I'm here; just thinking." I sighed, but quietly, so she couldn't hear (am I, like, the most considerate person in the whole wide world or what?).

"Oh, good. So what do you think—the gypsy and lace outfit, or not?"

"Not. You want to look sophisticated and elegant for Ruaraidh, not like a reject from a really bad seventies re-run. Go with the pink mini mod; that's the look that says what you want to say."

"I'm not exactly sure *what* I want to say," Holly waffled. She's been doing a lot of that lately, too. "But I suppose the pink mini does make me look older."

I know you were wondering how things are going between her and Ruaraidh of the eleven fingers, but there's not really much to tell. They haven't seen each other except for the one weekend at the beginning of March when Ruaraidh came down to meet her mom and stepdad. Holly said her mom kicked up a bit of a fuss 'cause she was dating a guy who was eighteen (she didn't seem to mind that he had an extra finger on his left hand, though), but Holly'll be sixteen in a couple of months so it's not really that big an age difference. I mean, Devon turned nineteen in February, and you don't see Brother or Mom saying anything about me dating him. Then again, I will be seventeen in just two weeks (woo-hoo! Can't wait!), and I *am* very mature for my age and all.

Anyhoo, Holly and I talked about what she was going to wear when she went up to see Ruaraidh, and what she would say, and what he was likely to say back to her, and how she should respond to that, and what he would think of the latest sweater she'd knitted him (she's up to five now. I'm still trying to knit my darling Devon a lump-free scarf, but I've only got a couple of inches that actually look like scarf), what she was going to do when he kissed her, and all that other stuff you have to talk about when you've been away from your BF for months and months and months. You know how she is—obsessed! It's hard to get a word in when she's going on and on and on about Ruaraidh, but I'm sure that's just because she misses him so much.

Aren't you glad I'm not like that?

Not that I could be, since Dev has been soooo attentive (*fan self*). Because he's perfect, and because I'm a GF extraordinaire, I called him after Holly went over what she should say to Ruaraidh for the fifth time. Five is my limit—indulging in conversation practice more than that makes you sound stilted, like you've been . . . well, practicing.

"Snuggle bunny!" I said when Devon answered his cell phone (they call them mobile phones here, which I guess makes sense, because what exactly *is* a cellular?). "I'm back, and guess what? I'm going to have a baby!"

Devon made an odd sort of choking noise. "You're . . . you're *what*? But we haven't . . . You told me you wanted to wait . . . You're still a . . . Is it Fang? Is that it? You told *me* no, but you've been shagging my best mate?"

Whoa! I wanted to tease him, but suddenly Devon sounded all pissed off and hurty and stuff. "Of course I haven't . . . *you know* . . . with Fang. He's my best friend, too." (Besides, you, of course. You're my BFF, but Fang's a sweetie and he's my best guy friend. Next to Devon, but Dev doesn't count because he's a BF, and BFs rank higher than just a guy friend. Where was I? Oh, yeah. Devon.) "I would never do that to you, Devon; you know that! I'm the one who told you that you couldn't date any other girls if we were going to go together, so why do you think I'd tell you that and not do the same?"

"But . . . you said you're pregnant—"

I made a face at the phone. I know it was a teensy bit mean, but I was a little insulted by what he said. You know that my main concern with him all along has been that he's the flirtiest guy on two legs, and I wasn't ab-sopositively sure he could just be with me without going for another girl, but he has, which is why he's the perfect Mr. Emily. "I never said that, you great big silly pants. I said I was going to have a baby. And I am. From Wednesday to Friday; then I have to turn it back in to Horseface Naylor."

Devon said something I'm not going to repeat because I know you don't like potty-mouth words, then heaved a big sigh. "Oh, the pregnancy-prevention doll. I forgot they are doing that at Gobotty now. They didn't when I was there."

"It's going to be fun. Brother is already threatening to go away if I leave my baby lying around so it annoys him. And just think, while I have the baby, you'll be a daddy!"

Devon swore (I'm going to have to punish him for it, oh, yes, I am!). "It's only for a few days, I don't suppose I'll have much to do with it."

"Sure you will! I have to help you on Wednesday pick out what to wear to Paris, and then on Thursday you promised to hang out with me, so we'll have lots of quality baby time together. I have to turn it in on Friday afternoon before I fly to Paris. Everyone else is turning theirs in on Saturday, but because I'm leaving early, Mom asked the school if I can get rid of it on Friday. Horseface was not happy, but ha ha ha ha," I said as I twirled around my room. "I'm going to be spending two weeks in the most romantic city in the world with the most romantic, nummy, totally snogworthy guy in the whole world, and she has to stay home and download baby data."

"One week," Devon said carefully.

"What?" I asked, stopping the twirling (it was making

me a bit barfy—you know how easily I get dizzy). "What?"

"I promised Dad I'd go fishing with him, so I'll only have one week to spend in Paris with you, Emily."

My heart, a previously happy, GF-to-a-fabulous-BF heart, a madly-in-love heart, a heart filled to the rim with thoughts of all the wonderful ways I was going to kiss Devon in Paris, dried up into a shriveled little thing that looked like your great-grandma Mabel's ears before she died. And you know how icky 108-year-old ears can look. "Noooooo!"

"I'm really sorry, love, but things haven't been too good between Dad and me since Mum kicked him out. I know you'll be busy with the intensive French classes and outings, and won't miss me at all that first week."

"Of course I'll miss you," I said, thinking about going into full pout mode. I decided not to only because a pout doesn't translate well on the phone. "The whole reason I was looking forward to Paris is because you'll be staying in a really nice hotel, and I can stay with you if I want, and we won't have the parental units breathing down our backs every second and coming up with feeble excuses to interrupt us while they make sure we're not having sex. Besides," I said, taking a really deep breath, my tummy going all woobidy at the thought of what I was going to say, "my birthday is on the eighteenth, and I was going to let you give me a special birthday present."

"Another one?" Devon asked. "I already bought all of the items on the list you gave me."

I gnawed my lip. I know it's bad to gnaw when you're trying to have happy, plump, kissy lips, but sometimes a girl just has to give in and gnaw, and this was one of those times. "This is something special. Something you'll like, too."

"Not another Motörhead CD?" Devon asked suspiciously.

"No. *Special*," I said, wondering if I had to spell it out to him. "Really special. Something you've never had before. Well, you've had it, probably, although I don't know for sure, but I'm almost positive you have, not that I care if you have, because that was before you gave me my ring, but I haven't, and that's what's special."

There was a silence on the other end of the phone for a couple of seconds, then Devon asked, "Another *Buffy* DVD?"

"No!" I rolled my eyes. I mean, sheesh! He was a guy! He was supposed to know what I was talking about without me having to say it, right? "S-P-E-C-I-A-L. Picture the scene—you and me, alone in your hotel room on my birthday. At night. Just the two of us—"

"Are you talking about a romantic dinner?" Devon asked.

"—just the two of us," I said, kind of grinding the words between my teeth. How on earth was Devon taking all those hard engineering classes if he couldn't figure out something simple like this? Obviously I was going to have to give him a bigger hint. "The two of us . . . with no clothes on."

9

Five more seconds of silence. "You want to play strip poker?"

"SEX!" I yelled into the phone. "We're going to have sex!"

"We are?" Devon asked; then he worked the shocked tone out of his voice, and quickly said, "Oh. I didn't realize you'd changed your mind. Erm . . . are you sure, Emily? You were awfully adamant when you made no sex one of the terms of our dating."

"That was because we hadn't been boyfriend and girlfriend before, and I didn't want you calling me names like Aidan did when he thought I was going to put out but I didn't."

"Emmy, love," he said in that wonderful breathy voice that made me go all girly. "You know I'd never do anything like that to you. I agreed to your terms because I'm mad about you just the way you are. You're smart and sexy and funny, and you put other people's feelings ahead of your own."

I stopped kissing my pillow with the iron-on of Devon's face that I had printed from his picture. "That last bit was too much, buster."

"Was it?" He sighed, then did a little laugh. "I wondered if it was, but I figured it was worth a shot."

"I might not be Saint Emily, but I suppose if you really, really, really have to go with your dad so you can stand around killing innocent fish for a week, I won't be too heartbroken. I'll only cry for three days straight. And I'll write really bad poetry about my heart breaking. But that's OK. I'll survive. *Somehow.*"

"That was about as subtle as *my* attempt." He laughed, and despite the fact that I was really disappointed that we wouldn't have two weeks together in Paris, I felt pretty happy. I had told him the News, and he sounded happy about it, not that I thought he wouldn't be, because he sometimes got, you know, *that way* when we were kissing, so I know he wants to and all.

We talked for a bit more about what we were going to do in Paris (he's going to take me to a really hot nightclub!); then Brother barged into my room and asked me if I'd like him to set up an IV line so I could ingest my meals intravenously in order to talk continuously on the phone without ever taking a break and giving someone else a chance to receive a phone call. Fathers! I'm telling you, if he weren't paying for me to go to live it up in Paris with Devon—I mean, to attend an intensive French class—I'd tell him a thing or two.

Gotta go—my toenails are done and I want to give Devon his good-night call. He's so nummy! I'm so happy! Life just can't possibly get any better than it is now, except after The Night, of course. Everything will be better after that!

Hugs and kissies,
~Em

Subject: Re: OMG! OH, MY GOD!
From: Em-the-enforcer@englandrocks.com
To: Dru@seattlegrrl.com
Date: 5 April 2004 7:58 pm

Dru wrote:
> *You're going to do it? IT??? With Devon? OHMIGOD!*
> *You have to tell me everything! What are you going*
> *to wear? What are you going to do? No, wait, I know*
> *what you're going to do, I mean, how are you going*
> *to act? OMG! This is so major! I haven't even thought*
> *of doing it with Timothy, and here you are making a*
> *sex date! OMG, OMG, OMG!*

Sheesh, Dru, you don't have to go all *Springer* on me!
It's not that big of a deal.

Well, OK, it is; it's the biggest thing that has ever happened to me, and that includes the night Devon gave me
my ring, which up till now has been the biggest thing,
but don't you think that *doing it* qualifies as the biggest
thing? I do. Getting into Harvard would be close, but I
really do think this is bigger.

OK, I just had a spaz attack thinking about how this
will be the most important moment ever, the moment
when I know Devon loves me more than anything else,
the moment when I'm sure that we're absolutely perfect
for each other and that we'll spend the rest of our lives
together. So in order to remain sane, we have to stop
talking about it. 'Cause otherwise I'm really going to

freak out, and you know that's never pretty.

What if I don't do it right? What if I'm, like, bad? What if Devon hates it with me and is too nice to tell me? What if I don't like it? What if he looks at me and doesn't get *that way*? What he if thinks I'm too ugly to do it with? OHMIGOD, I'll die! I'll drop down dead right there in his hotel room, ugly, naked, and still a virgin, and Mom and Brother will have to come to France, and they'll KNOW! They'll know I was too ugly and horrible at it for Devon to do it with me, and if I wasn't already dead, I'd die again, and they'll probably put it on my headstone.

Here lies Emily, so ugly no one would do it with her.

Aaaaaaaaaaack!

All right. No more sex talk. None. Zippo. Zilch. *Nada. Rien!* (that means *nothing* in French).

So, for a nonsex topic, let me tell you about . . . um . . . my baby. OK, there's a bit of sex there, but only pretend sex, not real sex, not the kind of real sex where if the love of your life, a guy so nummy you want to drool whenever you see him, decides you're just too horrible to do it with, you'll die. Not that kind of sex.

We had our first day of baby boot camp today at school. Horseface Naylor (yes, she still hates me, although I don't know why; I'm a perfect Saint Emily in her class. Well, except for the time I made whinnying noises when she walked into the library. And the time she found that cartoon of her that Holly and I had been drawing. And the day I slipped up and called her Miss Neighsmore. But other than that, I've been perfect) . . . what was I saying?

Oh, the baby stuff. Horsie is taking over the week of baby training.

"Becoming a parent is not a decision you should take lightly," she said, glaring at me. I couldn't tell if she was glaring at me just on general principle, or if she knew I was planning on doing *it* with Devon in a couple of weeks. "Creating a child is an action that will have an effect on you for the remainder of your life. In order to bring home just how important it is that you consider the ramifications of engaging in sexual contact, Gobottle School has gone to the enormous expense of purchasing the very latest in realistic baby simulators, which you will all receive tomorrow afternoon before you leave school."

I waggled my eyebrows at Holly. That always makes her laugh.

"The LuvMyBaby units are programmed to wake up randomly day and night, alerting you to their needs by crying. The computer inside each unit monitors how you care for the baby. One-third of this class's grade will consist of how well you care for the baby over a seventy-two-hour period."

I raised my hand. "How loud is the baby? My father said he's going to stay with a friend if he has to listen to a pretend baby cry all night long."

"The LuvMyBaby creators have included actual recorded cries of babies in each unit." Her lips twisted into a grim smile. "It is a very realistic, very effective cry. I would suggest you purchase a pair of earplugs for your father."

"Not to mention one for me," I said to Holly.

Horseface whirled around and pinned me with a glare that would have killed a lesser girl. "If you handle the unit too roughly, or if you do not support its neck, your actions will be recorded. If you do not change the doll when it needs changing, the computer will note your lack of actions. If you do not feed the baby at the appropriate intervals, it will be so recorded on the computer chip. If you neglect, abuse, or mistreat the unit in any way, the computer will know, and ultimately"—her grim smile turned particularly evil—"*I* will know. Your grade will suffer accordingly."

"There goes the earplug plan." I sighed.

"Can we hire a baby-sitter?" Snickerer Ann asked. Yes, she and Snickerer Bee are still snickerers, and they're still snotty to me. I just ignore them. They're *so* juvie.

"No. Once you assume responsibility for your baby, you can't leave it with anyone else. Each of you will receive a tamperproof wristband with a plastic key attached that you insert before feeding and tending to the baby. The key signals the computer that care is being given; thus only the assigned parent may quiet the baby."

"No baby-sitter?" I whispered to Holly. "Is she serious? Devon is going to take me to a movie on Thursday! I figured I'd get my mom to take care of the baby for me, but I can't do that if it's going to ruin my grade."

"Maybe it won't be that bad," Holly whispered back to me. "If you just missed a couple of hours, that wouldn't do much harm, would it?"

I waved my hand in the air again. Miss Neigh-Neigh rolled her eyes and ignored me until I added a little snap to the wave. "What is it, Williams?"

"So how important is this baby-care stuff?"

She made a kind of growl that I thought was really uncalled-for. I mean, are teachers supposed to growl at students? That's got to be against some sort of law. "I have just spent the last ten minutes explaining how important it is. One-third of your grade hinges on your success with the babies, and those of you who are facing a lackluster grade thus far in the semester"—she narrowed her eyes at me like she was making a point or something—"will find the only way to pass is to have a nearly perfect response rate with the babies."

"But what if someone had a really important date and she had to leave the baby with her mom, and the baby cried during that time, and the parent wasn't there with her key to turn the baby off? How bad would that be, grade-wise?" I figured it wouldn't hurt to ask.

"Failure," Horseface said, snapping the word like it was something brittle and she was . . . um . . . something snappy. A turtle, yeah, that's it. She said it just like she was one of those snapping turtles. "Such a blatant act of child negligence would result in a failing grade."

"Oy," I said, trying to think of how I was going to explain to Devon that our baby would have to come with us to the movie.

"Any further questions, Williams?"

"I don't suppose I can request to have a nonfussy

baby?" I asked, thinking that if it was quiet, maybe I could stuff it into my big canvas book bag so no one would know I had it with me.

Horsewoman's lips peeled back in another smile. It really was a gruesome sight. "I assure you, Williams, I will do everything within my power to see to it you have the doll you deserve."

That sounded an awful lot like a threat, don't you think? I bet you she gives me an *über*cranky baby because she hates me. Which means I'm going to have to be the best mom there ever was, because I refuse to let her screw up my chances of getting into Harvard just because I had the Demon Seed baby.

The rest of the class was spent creating a budget for what it costs to raise a kid. You wouldn't believe how much money it is just to go to the hospital to have one! I'm going to have to marry someone really rich, which, luckily, Devon is. Not that I love him for his money, you understand. I love him 'cause he's all nummy and stuff. I just can't wait until my birthday, when we get to do all sorts of wicked things to each other, assuming, of course, that he wants to do them to me . . . Rats! I'm doing it again!

No sex talk, no sex talk, no sex talk.

Tomorrow we get to see the dolls and learn basic baby care; then the keys are bound to our wrists and it's hello, Mommy for the next three days. Wish me luck. With Horseface at the controls, I'm willing to bet I get the evilest of all the babies.

17

> *So! You'll never guess what happened. Sukey and I*
> *were coming out of Biology, and I ran right into Andy*
> *Forrest (you remember him; he used to be all chunky,*
> *and was on the chess team), and he said hi, and I*
> *said, like, hi (only really cool), and Sukey did the nose-*
> *snorty thing she does. And later, when we were at*
> *Dairy Queen for lunch, she told me that she heard that*
> *Andy had gotten some girl pregnant. Andy Forrest!*
> *Some girl! Pregnant! OMG!*

Boy, you just don't know about people, do you? Andy sat next to me in third grade, and he didn't seem at all like the kind of guy who would go around *breeding*. Oh, hey, what happened when you told Mr. Barnes that you wanted to do your work experience at the modeling agency rather than Nordstrom? Did he OK it? That is so cool that you talked the agency into letting you do your two weeks WE with them. Just think of all those modelly-type people floating around. And photographers! I just bet you one of the photographers sees you and wants to make you an instant model!

Gotta go and finish this baby budget. We have to plan for eighteen years! Man, if I have the three kids I'm planning on having, I'm going to be broke unless I marry rich. Something to think about, huh?

Hugsies,
~Em

Subject: Jack Williams
From: Em-the-enforcer@englandrocks.com
To: Dru@seattlegrrl.com
Date: 6 April 2004 3:22 pm

Just got home. It's a boy! I've named him Jack. So far so good. No crying, but boy, howdy, these things sure are lifelike. Mom came to pick me up because I had to get the car seat and bag o' baby stuff, and she freaked when she held it. She said they weighted the head and made the neck all wobbly just like a real baby's.

Hs and Ks,
~Em the mom

Subject: Crap
From: Em-the-enforcer@englandrocks.com
To: Dru@seattlegrrl.com
Date: 6 April 2004 3:26 pm

Spoke too soon. He's crying. It's really annoying. Gotta go. Can't type with one hand while holding the bottle in his mouth.

Subject: More crap!
From: Em-the-enforcer@englandrocks.com
To: Dru@seattlegrrl.com
Date: 6 April 2004 3:47 pm

Still crying. Have fed, changed diaper (he just wets, thank God—couldn't cope with fake poop), patted on back. I'm running out of things to do. Bet I got the defective model.

Horseface is evil.

Subject: Want a baby?
From: Em-the-enforcer@englandrocks.com
To: Dru@seattlegrrl.com
Date: 6 April 2004 3:54 pm

Adoption is clearly my next option if JACK DOESN'T SHUT UP!!!

Subject: Criminy dutch!
From: Em-the-enforcer@englandrocks.com
To: Dru@seattlegrrl.com
Date: 6 April 2004 8:13 pm

OK, I'm convinced: no kids for me, not until I am making oodles of money and can afford a nanny, 'cause I am clearly not cut out for this mom stuff. Jack cried for a half hour solid! Nothing I did would shut him up. When I took him to Mom, she just shrugged and said, "Welcome to the world of motherhood."

This is a parent plot, you know. I was supposed to meet

Holly at the library tonight, but couldn't because I had to take care of Jack (twice since I got home!). She got a boy also (she named hers Iain, which is Ruaraidh's middle name), but hers only cried once so far. I was talking to her while I was walking around with Jack—I had to keep patting his back, because Chloe T told us that the babies have sensors to know when you touch them, and patting sometimes works to shut them up—and he was crying so hard I couldn't even hear her tell me what she decided to wear to Scotland.

This is going to be a long three days.

Oh, hey, I meant to tell you about Aurora! Bess brought her home. She's a Wiccan (Aurora, not Bess—Bess is too into her radical causes to ever do girly Wiccan stuff like burn incense and meditate and things). Anyway, I wandered into the library and found Bess and Aurora sitting on the floor around a circle made of tulip petals.

"What's up?" I asked, plopping myself and Jack onto the couch. Mom had found a plastic baby carrier at a thrift shop, and bought it for me to transport Jack, which is really cool, because I don't think anyone else has one, although Holly said she was going to get one of the baby backpacks for her Iain. "Doing some weirdo radical feminist flower thing?"

"It's an invocation to the goddess, you boob. This is my sister, Emily," Bess told her friend. "The one I mentioned. Em, this is Aurora. She's a Wiccan."

I made mean eyes at Bess for the boob comment before I realized what she said. I looked at Aurora. "Wiccan? That's, like, a really cool witch, right?"

Aurora smiled. She had braces, but even with them, she had a nice smile. "Something like that, yes."

"Coolio! My room is haunted. Think you can do something about it?"

"Haunted?" she asked, doing an eyebrow wiggle. "Haunted how? Poltergeist? Cold spot? Energy balls?"

"Underwear ghost," I answered. She just stared at me, so I figured I'd better explain more in case she thought I was, like, all insane or something. "It likes to throw my undies all over the room. I've tried everything—taping the drawer shut, mousetraps, putting big heavy books on top of the undies—but nothing works. Every couple of days I find my undies all over the room. I think the dresser is haunted by the ghost of an underwear pervert."

"Oh. I haven't . . ." She blinked a couple of times. I didn't make a big thing out of her not believing me, because, you know, it really *is* strange. ". . . I haven't ever heard of a haunted dresser, but I suppose anything is possible."

"Do you think you can exorcise it, or whatever you do to an underwear ghost?" I asked. "Can you hold a séance and tell it to stop fondling my bras? 'Cause it's getting a bit old having to come in and pick up stuff all the time."

"You could just use another drawer," Bess said.

"That is *so* not the point! I should be able to use all the drawers, not just the bottom three! Besides, there isn't enough room for everything in just three drawers."

"If you wouldn't spend every cent you had on clothes,

you'd have plenty of room—" Bess started to say, but you know her, she's all "You should be giving your money to needy causes," and yet *she* manages to buy new stuff all the time. And Monk (he's back—what I thought was a breakup was just him going off to some meditation center for two weeks) always buys her CDs and stuff, too, so really, she has no right to pick on me.

Rats. Lost my place again. Um . . . oh, Aurora.

"Can you do something about it?" I interrupted Bess to ask her. "Please?"

"Well . . ." Aurora looked kind of worried. "I won't do a séance. I don't believe in contacting those who have gone beyond. But I can conduct a cleansing ritual to dispel any negative energy that might be held within your room, if you think it will help."

"Coolio!" I said. "Can you do it now?"

She shook her head. "I need some supplies. I could do it Thursday night."

"Excellent. Oh, wait, I've got a date that night. Poop."

"A date?" Bess asked, throwing a tulip petal at me. "What about Baby Screams a Lot?"

"Jack will come with us," I said, figuring that I'd just make sure that I had fed and changed him before we went to the movie. "Could we maybe do the cleaning thing before dinner?"

"I suppose I could, although it's most effective by moonlight."

So we settled that she's coming over Thursday afternoon to do the undie-ghost cleaning, yay!

Oops! Gotta go. Have stupid homework to do, and then I have to call Devon and let him know that Jack is coming with us on Thursday. I think maybe I'll go over to his house tomorrow, just to introduce him to Jack. It'll be good for him, don't you think?

Hugs and kisses,
~Em

Subject: Re: The boob fondle
From: Em-the-enforcer@englandrocks.com
To: Dru@seattlegrrl.com
Date: 8 April 2004 4:20 pm

Dru wrote:
> *his hand right there on my chest! Like he had the right*
> *to, or something! And then I said, "Liam, you are so*
> *not my type; I'd rather French-kiss a donkey than you!"*
> *And he squeezed my boob! So I hauled off and belted*
> *him right in the snot locker. Gave him a bloody nose,*
> *too. There was blood everywhere, and I got to tell*
> *Mrs. Taylor what he did, hahahahahahah!*

Oh, man, I wish I had been there to see that. How very cool that you gave him a bloody nose, although I suppose if the blood splattered on your white Candies, that would take a bit of the fun out of the situation. Try club soda— that's what Mom uses for everything. And go, you, for not taking any sort of sexual harassment! We studied harassment earlier this year. Turns out all sorts of things you wouldn't think were harassment really are, stuff like a guy kissing you without you really wanting him to. I bet I could sue Aidan for sexual harassment if I wanted to! I mean, he did keep trying to grab my hand and drag it over to his thingy. If that's not harassment, I just don't know what is.

> *Sorry to hear you aren't getting much sleep with Jack.*
> *The LuvMyBabies that we had were v1.20, which I*
> *guess was the really early model, because I didn't have*
> *any trouble with Sarah. She slept through both nights.*
> *And also, it only took a little bit of time before she'd*
> *stop crying, not the half hour or more that Jack is*
> *doing. Did you ask your teacher if she set something*
> *up wrong?*

Oh, I'm so not going to do that; she'll just make him cry nonstop. I got three hours' sleep last night—three hours! How am I supposed to go to school and be intelligent and everything when I've only had three hours of sleep? I have two tests on Friday! I can't study for them if I'm so groggy from lack of sleep that I can't even remember what it is I'm studying for.

> *Speaking of that, what did Devon say when you*
> *brought Jack by? Was he a good daddy?*

25

Ha! Oh, chick, was that ever an experience! I went over to Devon's house last night to help him pick out stuff to wear in Paris—well, not really, because he has good taste and all, but it sounds very GF-y to say you're going over to your BF's to help him pick out clothes, so that's what I said I was going to do, but once I got there all we did was watch *Big Brother* on his new widescreen TV.

Right in the middle of it Jack went off. Now, here's the thing—I told you that Devon's parents have separated, right? It's kind of sad because I liked his dad a lot the one time I met him. He looks a bit like Jack Lemmon, and he has a wicked funny sense of humor (which kind of embarrassed Devon, but you know how it is with parents—what you think is awful all your friends think is funny). Anyway, Devon's mom has been kind of weepy and sad and stuff since Christmas. Devon let me in last night, so his mom didn't see me and Jack; she just yelled hello from the other room.

So Jack starts crying right as we're watching *Big Brother* upstairs in the den. All of a sudden his mom burst into the room, her eyes all big and bulgy like Ricky's on *I Love Lucy*.

"I heard a baby," she said in rush. Her eyes got even Ricky-er when she saw Devon holding Jack, patting him on the back (I was showing Devon how you have to rub his back to soothe him). "Good God! Emily, you had a baby? I had no idea you were even pregnant! Who—that is, who is the . . . erm—"

Devon got this *überly* wicked look in his eye (just like

his dad's), and, totally deadpan, said, "Mum, you *know* Emily is my girl. Come on in and meet Jack. I bet you never thought you'd have a grandson quite like him."

Devon's mom clawed at her throat for a second, her mouth opening and closing like one of those goldfish you had as she gasped, "Grand . . . grand . . ." Then she just keeled over right there in the hallway!

For one horrible minute I thought we'd killed her with shock, but she started moaning just as Devon shoved Jack at me and went to help her. He thought it was pretty funny later on (after he got her up off the floor), but he e-mailed me this morning that she read him the riot act after I left. Evidently she *didn't* think it was funny. I sure wish Devon lived with his dad instead. I bet he would have laughed.

Oops! Gotta run; Aurora is here. I'll fill you in later on how the deghosting went (not to mention the date with Devon).

Big smoochy kisses,
~Em

Subject: You will NOT believe the day I've had!
From: Em-the-enforcer@englandrocks.com
To: Dru@seattlegrrl.com
Date: 9 April 2004 5:49 pm

Why is it that normal things never happen to me? You know, like you breaking your leg skiing last year? That was normal. Other people break their legs skiing. But how many people do you know with an honest-to-Pete poltergeist running around playing with their underwear? How many people do you know who get kicked out of a movie theater? How many people do you know who get stuck in the middle of the feckin' wilderness for three hours while in ENGLAND, a country that's been civilized since the beginning of time?

Crap. I have to make this short—as soon as Mom recovers from the accident, she has to drive me to the school so I can turn in Baby Ruin My Life. But first things first—I have to tell you about the ghost. Aurora came by yesterday afternoon to un-ghost my room. She brought all sorts of smelly candles and herbs and stuff, and set them all out around the room, most of them concentrated around the dresser from hell.

"The first thing I do," Aurora said as she set a brand-new white candle on top of the dresser, "is anoint the candle with spirit oil."

"Spirit oil?" I asked, watching as she drizzled a little bit of oil on the candle. "What's that?"

"It's oil mixed with pennyroyal, sulfur, mullein, and yarrow. The pennyroyal provides protection from evil in your personal space, the sulfur prevents a being from having power over you, the mullein keeps away demons and nightmares, and the yarrow clears the space of any evil spirits."

"Wow, all that in one handy little oil," I said. "Does it really work?"

Here's a little hint from me to you—if you ever ask a

Wiccan to come to your house and deghost your under-wear drawer, do not, no matter how skeptical you are, ask if it really works, 'cause whoever it is doing the magic stuff is bound to get annoyed.

"Magic is not a precise science," Aurora said in a miffed tone. "Magic is the act of altering consciousness by your will. As people, very little in our lives is in our control, which is why our will to shape and change our life force, and those forces around us, is our only tool. If you do not believe, the magic will not work."

"Sorry," I said quickly, not wanting her to get so ticked off she left without taking care of my ghost. "I'm almost absolutely positive that I believe."

She shot me a look that was just like the one Bess was giving me (part eye-roll, part disgusted curled-lip sneer), and went to each of the windows to sprinkle salt.

"Um . . . why salt?" I asked as she moved over to the door. "I thought it was supposed to be bad luck to spill salt? Are you trying to annoy the ghost so it leaves?"

"If that's all it took to get it to leave, you'd certainly have done it long ago," Bess said snottily. Which explains why I have petitioned Mom and Brother three times now to formally disavow Bess.

"Salt provides protection against evil spirits entering your room," Aurora said.

"That's nice and all, but the ghost is already here," I pointed out.

She didn't say anything to that, just took out a big blue

stone bowl and started putting stuff into it. I peered over her shoulder to see what she was doing.

"This is garlic, dried thistle, clove, sage, and peppermint," she said. "I will light it, and it will drive out the spirit. Bess?"

Bess came forward with a lighter and lit a small stick. Aurora wedged the stick into the dried herbs, stirring it around until they started to smoke. Then she walked all over the room, stopping at the dresser to wave the smoke into each of the opened drawers. "We come here in peace and understanding. By the name of the Eternal Lord and the Eternal Lady, we bid thee to part. By the name of the Eternal Lady and Eternal Lord, we consecrate this space. By the spirit within us, let nothing but joy linger here."

"Amen," I said, feeling like I should say something, except I didn't know any Wiccan stuff to say. "Is this it? When will I know if the ghost is gone?"

She set the bowl down in the open top drawer, right between my Wonderbra and that jogging bra I never wear because it makes my boobs flop around. The herbs were smoking something awful, filling up the room with herb smoke, so I went to open up a window.

"No, you must keep the windows closed or it won't work," Aurora said quickly. "We must wait until the herbs have finished burning; then we will take them outside and bury the ashes."

I waved my hand in the air, trying to flag the smoke out of my face. Bess started coughing deep, her icky-sounding asthma cough. My eyes stung as I started to cough, too. The smoke was really nasty. No wonder it would drive a ghost out. "Bury—cough, cough—the ashes? Why—hack, wheeze—bury them?"

"Can't stay; need my inhaler," Bess gasped as she ran for the door.

Even Aurora started wheezing a bit. "We bury the ashes to return them to the Earth Mother. I will admit, this is a bit strong—" She bolted for the door.

I followed right on her heels, stopping just long enough to grab Jack before escaping. After Aurora caught her breath, she told me that when I went back into the room, I should feel a difference.

"Yeah, but what's going to happen to all my undies and other stuff in the dresser? They'll all smell like smoke. I hate smoky clothes! I'll have to wash everything, and I've got two tests tomorrow, and I'm supposed to fly to Paris tomorrow night. I don't have time to be washing clothes."

Bess dragged Aurora off to her room. Isn't that just like her?

"The smoke should clear soon," Aurora said over her shoulder.

"Great," I told Jack, who was being quiet (did I tell you he has blue eyes just like Devon? Isn't that too fabu?). "It should clear soon. Do you see what happens when you have a sister? This is why you're an only child."

I went down to the library to do some homework until Devon picked me up, which meant I had to sit in the same room as Brother when he was writing up a paper on garderobes or peons or whatever it is a medieval scholar does. And you know how he grunts when he writes. He also mutters Latin under his breath, and I defy anyone to study while someone grunts and speaks Latin in the same room. Martyr that I am, I went in and braved the Stare of the Unibrowed (still no luck with leaving pairs of tweezers lying conveniently around).

"You can lower your unibrow; I'm not here to bother you. Devon's picking me up in a couple of hours, but until then I have to do my homework in here because my underwear is being smoked."

"For any particular reason, or were you just in the underwear-smoking sort of mood?" Brother asked.

"It's because your eldest child has weird friends. Oh, poop, Jack, not now!"

"Out," Brother ordered, pointing to the door. "I'm working on an important bit of research into an anthropological problem during the early Middle Ages. I cannot draw logical conclusions into the origin of sutlers with that thing squalling."

I sighed and put my key into Jack's back. "I'm an outcast in my own home," I said as I left the library.

"One more reason not to engage in sexual intercourse until you're thirty," Brother yelled after me.

It took me forever to calm Jack down. I went into the kitchen where Mom was painting another ceramic bowl with scenes from the *Domesday Book* (can my family get any stranger?), and told her that Horseface clearly set

Jack up to deprive me of much-needed sleep and that she should write a really stern note to Mr. Krigon and tell him to fire her for harassment.

"It might not be sexual," I said as I walked around the kitchen patting Jack on the back, "but it sure is harassing me!"

"It'll be over tomorrow night," she said. "Should I put the section with William the Conqueror on the pickle tray or the nut bowl?"

"Gee, Mom, pickles or nuts, what a dilemma. Why not put him on a fruitcake plate and call it done?" I said with much inner snickering. Nut bowls! Pickle trays! Hoot!

"A fruitcake plate?" Mom set down her paintbrush and reached for the ceramic supply catalog. "I must have missed that. A fruitcake plate. That sounds like just the thing I need to complete the set. . . ."

I went back out and sat on the stairs until Jack shut up, then put him in his carrier and did some homework until Bess burst into the library all schitzy, like something awful had happened. She jumped up and down a couple of times, coughing and choking and waving her hands toward the stairs like she was a crazy mime. Brother looked at me, his unibrow raised. I looked at him. We both looked at Bess.

"I think she's insane," I told Brother. "You should probably have her locked up. For her own good, of course."

"Fire!" Bess finally spit out. "Em's underwear is on fire!"

"What?" I shrieked, and shoved her out of my way as I ran out the library and up the stairs. Brother wheezed and knee-cracked his way up the stairs after me. The door to my bedroom was open, with great, huge billows of smoke filling the hallway. Aurora was standing in front of the dresser with the tiny bathroom trash can, pouring water all over my dresser.

"I think it's out," she said when I stood in the middle of the room and wailed. Brother opened the windows and went over to the dresser to stare at the mess.

"I'm sorry, Emily," Aurora said. "I don't know what happened, but the herbs must have started smoldering in your things. . . ."

"Oh, great, just great!" I stomped over to my underwear drawer and looked in. All my things, all my lovely satin undies and matching bras, and my Wonderbra, and the naughty black lace undies I was saving for Devon (not for him to wear, silly, although—ahahahahahah—wouldn't that be funny to see him in them?), and my everyday undies, and the bras I don't like but don't want to throw out because they make my boobs look good, and all the other stuff in there was just one big, black, wet, mucky, scorched mess.

"I'm very sorry," Aurora said again. "I used a fireproof bowl. I don't know how it could have set fire to your clothes—"

"It's the ghost," I said, waving my hands around dramatically. I mean, what else could I do? "It's doing this on purpose. Well, it had just better watch out, because THIS MEANS WAR!"

After we dug everything out of the drawer and made sure the dresser wasn't burning (it wasn't, which is more or less absolute proof that the ghost was trying to get back at me for ousting it), and opened up all the windows to air the room, Mom told me she'd take me to buy new undies before I left for Paris.

By the time Devon came to take me to the movie, I was pretty wiped out, but you know me, trooper to the end! So I spritzed myself with perfume to hide the smoky smell (everything in my room smelled like burned bras and herbs), and gathered up Jack and off we went.

"You're not bringing Jack, are you?" Devon asked as I grabbed the car seat. "Can't you leave it with your mother for a couple of hours?"

"No! He's just a helpless baby!" I said, all outraged that he would think I was such a bad mother I would leave my only child with my mother. "He has to come with us."

Devon watched as I got the car seat in his backseat, strapped Jack in, and tossed in his carrier and bag o' stuff. Devon had just retipped his hair (blond on black is the *über*coolioest!), and was wearing all black, which makes him look like the nummiest nummymeister of all num-myland. "Ah. Well, I suppose as it'll be just the once, I'll survive."

His blue eyes were all laughy-like, which you know just melts me. I scooted up next to him in the car so he could put his hand on my leg while he drove (which he did, yay!), and asked, "How's your mom doing?"

"Fine, although she got a bit shirty about me going to Paris to see you."

My stomach wadded up into a tiny, dense stomach wad. "You're still coming, aren't you? For the week? You're not going to back out? Not when I'm ready to . . . you know? OHMIGOD, you are backing out! It's me, isn't it? You don't want to do it with me? Aaaaaaaaargh!"

The car swerved as I grabbed his arm and shook it, Devon swearing under his breath as he got us back onto the right side of the road (which is actually the left side, 'cause they drive on the left, but you know that, right? That the left is the right side here? Right? I mean, left? Oh, poop, never mind.). "Christ, Emily! You almost killed us!"

"That's all right; I'm going to die anyway because you don't want me."

"I do want you, I've wanted you ever since I met you, but you didn't want me to want you, so I didn't. And before you get yourself worked up, no, I'm not backing out of Paris. I'll be there the last week of your stay. And assuming we survive this trip to the cinema, I will be more than happy to do whatever you want me to do in Paris, so you can stop looking at me like I'm some sort of monster."

I sniffed back the tears that had started up. "You're sure you want me? I mean really, really want me? Because I wouldn't want to force you into anything."

36

He flashed one of his knee-melting grins at me. "I'd love to give you physical proof, but you'd probably slap me if I did."

OHMIGOD! He was talking THINGIE! Eeek!

After I got over his thingie comment—I peeked, but that's all—the rest of the ride to the movie theater we talked about what we were going to do in Paris (no, not *that!* You need your mind washed out with soap!). Devon promised to take me on a canal boat ride, whatever that is. Sounds romantic, huh? Anyway, we got to the theater, and because I'd just changed Jack, I figured he wouldn't go off, so rather than haul his bag and the carrier in and have to sit him next to us—not to mention have people staring because I was hauling a fake baby around—I dragged out my big canvas book bag.

"Are you supposed to do that?" Devon asked as I carefully (have to support Jack's neck) put him into the bag.

"As long as he's not abused, he'll be fine," I said, and (gently) set my purse on top of him so no one would see I had a baby stuffed into my bag.

Everything was fine until the previews began. Jack went off during one of them, which meant that EVERY-ONE in the theater heard.

"Crap, crap, crap! I'll be back," I hissed to Devon as I grabbed the book bag.

"Do you want me to come with you?" he asked. (Isn't he the best?)

"No, you stay here and tell me what I missed," I whispered to him, then glared at the people behind us who were snarling at me to shut Jack up. "I'm leaving! Sheesh! It's just a preview! Some people have no life!"

I hurried out of the theater to the lobby, pulling first my purse out of the bag, then Jack. Because I didn't want to walk back and forth across a busy movie theater lobby with a crying doll in my arms, I went into the women's bathroom and sat in a stall.

Just as I got him quieted down, a woman in a police uniform came in and knocked on my stall.

"Um," I said, because you know, what else do you say when a policewoman knocks on your stall?

Through the crack in the stall door I could see the policewoman was all grim-looking. "Would you please come out, miss? There has been a complaint regarding a child in your possession."

"A child?" I looked at where I had been stuffing Jack back into the book bag. "Oh, Jack. It's OK. He won't go off again. I didn't think he'd start crying while I was in the movie because I just fed and changed him before we left home, but my teacher is a sadist and she hates me, so she set him up to make my life a living hell. But he really, really shouldn't disturb anyone for a couple of hours. Promise."

"Miss, if you will just step out of the stall," the police-woman said.

Two of the concession ladies now stood behind her. "Good God, she has the poor thing in that bag again!" one gasped.

The other shrieked. The police woman lunged toward

38

my bag, grabbing it and jerking it out of my hands.

"Hey!" I yelled as I followed her out of the stall. "Stop that! If you jerk his head around it'll show up as abuse and I'll get in trouble!"

"You're a horrible, horrible girl," the second concession woman—the evil one—said as she put her arm around the first, who was sniffling like something terrible had happened. "You should have that poor innocent dear taken away from you!"

OK, so it took me a bit before I figured out what was going on, but at last I realized what the problem was—they thought Jack was real.

"It's a doll," I said, crossing my arms and watching as the policewoman carefully extracted Jack. The two concession women crowded around her, both making those weird faces women make when one of them has a baby and the others all coo over it.

The policewoman was the first one to realize I was telling the truth. Even so, she glared at me. I grinned back at her and held up Jack's key. "See? A doll."

"Young woman, I do not find this prank at all funny," she said.

The two concession ladies gasped together, then narrowed their eyes at me. "Not funny in the least. We don't want your type at the Piddleton Cinema Twelve," the evil concession woman said. "I shall inform Derek of your offense; you may be sure of that."

"Whatever," I said, all righteous because I didn't do anything wrong. "Can I have my doll back, please?"

The policewoman handed him back, but before she let me go, she made me stand there and listen to her lecture me about taking Jack out in public where people would misunderstand what I was doing.

By the time I got out of the bathroom, an old, fat, bald guy was talking with the evil concession woman. You guessed it; he came over and told me to leave, that he didn't want troublemakers in his cinema. I explained about Jack, but in the end I had to go in and get Devon (while Derek the Hun stood and watched me) and we left. But I made them give Devon his money back first, and I threatened to file a harassment charge against them.

That was yesterday—today Mom wrote me a note to leave school early, so we could go buy me new bras and undies. Holly and I are flying to Paris (doesn't that sound *über*coolio? Flying to Paris! We're so worldly!) tonight at nine. Holly's stepdad, Alan, had two freebie tickets to Paris; otherwise we'd have had to take the train tomorrow with everyone else, which would be kind of cool because I've never seen the Chunnel—that's the tunnel that connects England and France—but it's much more megacool to fly, don't you think? Anyway, Mom got me sprung early and we went to find some undies. She wanted to go to a town called Cirencester (another weirdo English name—it's pronounced si-ren-sest-er) to get more ceramic stuff, like she doesn't have enough now, but whatever, and promised to take me to the really cool shops there to buy undies and a few other things.

40

Well! We go, we shop, we buy undies (three new bras, a whole week's worth of undies, and I got a red satin bustier! More about that later.), and Mom goes nutso-cuckoo at the ceramic shop, and as we're heading home, we run smack-dab into a good old-fashioned Seattle-style traffic jam. There was a big accident with a truck and a couple of cars, and it shut the whole road toward Piddlesville down, so Mom got out the map and we headed off homeward via a back road.

Just as we were going past a row of stone houses, a duck ran out in front of the car, and Mom slammed the brakes on. I screamed, Jack started crying, and Mom swore up a blue streak as the car skidded on the mud in what seemed like slow motion just before we plowed into a tree at the side of the road.

"Are you all right?" Mom asked, sounding really shaky.

"Yeah, but I hope Jack didn't get hurt," I said as I undid my seat belt and climbed into the back of the car.

"Jack?" Mom started to laugh, kinda hysterically if you want to know the truth, and I was just thinking about slapping her when a couple of people ran out from one of the stone houses.

Turns out we were in a little village called Broughton Poggs. No, I am not kidding. It's this little nothing town, a bunch of stone houses on a road and a church, and that's pretty much it. No shops, no gas station, nothing. Luckily Mom had her cell phone, and she called up Brother and told him a duck had almost killed us, but we were fine, yadda yadda yadda. We ended up being there for three whole hours before Brother found us and rescued us from BP.

Anyway, by the time I got home, I had— Oh, poop. Gotta run; Mom's through explaining to Brother why she creamed the car. I'm supposed to be dropping Jack off with Horsewoman, but I think I'm going to get Brother to go to the local chemist (drugstore, remember?) first before it closes. I just realized that I don't have any nail polish that will go with the bustier. The Neighster can keep her hooves on a few extra minutes. I'll e-mail you from Paris!

Frenchy hugs and kisses,
~Em

Subject: [Fwd: Re: Geez, Em!]
From: EmInParis@parisstudy.com
To: Dru@seattlegrrl.com
Date: 10 April 2004 9:43 am

Dru wrote:
> *When you do something, you do it all the way! You're*
> *right. I don't know anyone else who would burn her*
> *underwear in order to get rid of a ghost. And that*
> *movie guy was just a poop. Was Devon mad that you*
> *guys had to leave early? You must be in Paris now; tell*
> *me what it's like! I wish I could be there with you!*
> *Wah! You're so lucky! You're in PARIS!!!!!!!!!!!!!!!*

There are times when I'm absopositively certain that God or whoever runs the universe hates me. And then there are times like this when I know it's true, because I have proof!

Yes, I'm in Paris (note temporary Paris addy). I'm here, Holly's here, Snickerer Bee is here (her mom and Holly's mom work together, and SB's mom thought the French school sounded like a good idea), and Jack is here.

Yes, Jack. My Baby Drive You Insane. Why, you must be asking? Why, oh, why did I drag a baby doll that cries at a drop of a hat with me on my *über*coolio trip to Paris? Why? Because Miss Horseface Neighster hates my guts and wants me to go crazy, that's why.

All right, I'm going to tell this properly if it kills me (and it probably will). Last night while I was e-mailing you about what a horrible day I'd been having, Mom—still a bit wigged out by the accident—convinced Brother to take me to the school so I could drop Jack off. Horsie was supposed to be there waiting to collect Jack, download the data, and release me from my baby bondage.

But she wasn't. We were only FORTY minutes late! And she had left! LEFT! Like she couldn't have waited? Ok, I admit, maybe it wasn't terribly smart to go nail polish shopping beforehand, but I didn't know she was going to leave!

She taped a note on the library door that said:

Emily Williams—as a student in my class, you know that punctuality is a quality I value greatly.

*Since you deemed it not worth your time to keep
the appointment you made with me—an appointment that forced me to rearrange my entire evening's schedule—to turn in your LuvMyBaby, I
assume that you desire to keep the doll with you
another night. Mrs. Milford will be in the school library tomorrow morning from nine o'clock until ten
to facilitate the return of the dolls. If you do not
return your LuvMyBaby during that time, you will be
responsible for its care during the two weeks of
spring break. I need not remind you that your grade
for the semester depends upon the data collected
by the LuvMyBaby—regardless of the duration of
time it is in your care.*

Now you know me: I'm not one to panic. I stopped
screaming after only five minutes, which I think is pretty
good, considering what Miss Horseface had just done to
me.

"What am I going to do?" I wailed, dragging Brother
out of the car so he could see the note. "I can't take Jack
with me to Paris! It'll ruin my trip! OHMIGOD!"

Brother pursed his lips and raised his unibrow. "Hmm.
I suppose your mother could return it for you tomorrow,
if you asked her nicely."

I grabbed his arms and shook him. How could he be
such a big scholar and not see the obvious? "I'm leaving
tonight! In three hours! I can't leave Jack all night; he'll
record that I abused him, and Horseface will fail me for

the class, and that will bring my GPA down even more, and I'll never get into Harvard with a crappy GPA!"

"Horseface?" Brother asked, looking all dopey, the way fathers can.

"Miss Naylor. Brother! What am I going to do!"

"Surely one bad grade can't ruin your GPA—" he started to say.

"It's not just one! She's given me awful grades all year! I've had to be doubly good in the other classes to make up for her grades, and another bad one will absolutely kill my chances at Harvard!"

"Perhaps if your mother took care of the baby until tomorrow—" he started to say.

I shoved my wrist under his nose. "She can't! The key is hot-wired so if the band is taken off my wrist, the doll knows. It's to keep us from having someone else watch the baby. I'm doomed!" I tossed my hands up and stormed off to the car. "Either I have to take a crappy grade and ruin the whole, entire rest of my life, or I have to take Jack with me to Paris. I hate my life!"

"Calm down, Emily; there's no sense in getting upset over something so trivial," Brother said as he got into the car.

"Trivial!" I gasped.

"Trivial," he said in that end-of-discussion voice. "I don't believe that your GPA will suffer as greatly as you claim, but if you are convinced of it, then you have two choices. Either you take the doll with you to Paris, or you contact Miss Naylor this evening, apologize for your tardiness, and politely request that she take the doll before you leave for the airport."

"You're a genius," I yelled, and kissed his cheek (he deserves it once in a while).

As it turns out, he wasn't that much of a genius. The whole time I packed, Mom tried calling Miss Naylor, but there was no answer. We even went by her house on the way to the airport, but the woman next door said she'd gone off to the Cotswolds for spring break. WAH!

So there I was three hours later, standing in the middle of Heathrow Airport with Jack, the baby carrier, my luggage, and Jack's bag. Could life get any worse?

"This is so unfair," I sniveled to Mom. "Can't you call up the school and explain to them what happened? Can't you tell them this isn't my fault? Can't you tell them it's illegal or something to make me take care of a fake baby for two whole weeks?"

"I'm afraid they're not going to see it that way," Mom said. She patted me on the arm as I fought back some pity-party tears. "I'll try to get hold of the headmaster for you. If he says you can cut the bracelet off, I'll call you."

"Thanks," I said, as miserable as I possibly could be, but what was I supposed to do? Mom couldn't take Jack or I'd fail the class. I couldn't leave Jack behind or I'd fail the class. I couldn't take him to Paris and ignore him, or I'd fail the class. It was Jack or my grades, and I've worked too hard to keep my grades up to toss them for a couple of weeks of UTTER AND COMPLETE BLISS.

I have the worst life of anyone I know.

People looked kind of strangely at me as Holly and I checked in, but no one said anything to me until we were on the plane. The flight attendant came over as I was clutching Jack's carrier to my chest.

"I'm sorry," she said as she looked at a list. "I don't see that you've purchased a ticket for your baby."

She wanted me to buy a ticket for Jack? I was so tired from lack of sleep (which, I'd like to point out, is all Jack's fault) that I stared at her until Holly nudged me. "Oh. It's not . . . This isn't a real baby. It's fake, see?"

"A fake baby!" she yelled, loud enough that everyone sitting around us could hear her.

I flipped Jack over and pulled up his baby tee to show the key slot in his back. "Fake."

"Oh. Why—" She waved her hand around.

"School thing," I said, and tried to pretend that everyone wasn't staring at us. My first trip by myself, my first trip to Paris where I was going to meet my boyfriend, and I get stuck hauling a fake baby doll around. Em the doll freak, yes, sir, that's me.

I hope you're crying for me, because I had a good bawl in the bathroom on the airplane. Holly did her best to cheer me up, but she wasn't the one who was damned to have Baby Screw Up Your Life with her during her whole fabulous time in Paris.

"Maybe it won't be so bad," she said. "Maybe you can look at this as a unique opportunity to find out what sort of a mother you will be."

"I know what sort of mother I will be," I said grumpily

(the grumpiness was *so* justified). "I will be the sort of a mother who has enough money to hire a nanny so she can spend two glorious weeks alone in Paris with the man of her dreams; that's the sort of mother I'll be."

Holly just smiled. She was all dreamy and happy because she'd had two fabu days with Ruaraidh and was still in Scottish Hottie Happyland. "I know it's hard, Em, but you shouldn't let this ruin Paris. Maybe Jack will settle down and you won't notice he's there. Probably you'll forget—"

Just as she spoke, Jack went off. I sighed and stood up to get him out of the overhead bin (the stewardess wouldn't let me hold him during takeoff). Everyone in the plane snickered and pointed at me as I hauled him down to feed and change him. A couple of people even took pictures of me, which wasn't too bad because I had taken the time to put on my going-to-Paris makeup (straight out of Paris *Vogue*!).

"What were you saying about not noticing he's here?" I asked Holly as I fed Jack his bottle of water.

She grinned. "Sorry. I still think it's better if you try to turn this into a positive experience rather than moping about it. I think if you looked at it in the right way, you'd see that it might be fun to have a baby in Paris."

Yeah, right, and maybe monkeys will fly out of my butt. I didn't say that, of course, because next to you, Holly is my best friend, but I thought it. *A lot*. The entire way over to Paris, which was only about forty minutes. I thought it would take hours or something, but it didn't! France is, like, right there next to England. Kind of weird, huh?

Anyway, we got off the plane, went through customs—and can I say how happy I am I don't speak French? I don't want to know what all the customs guys were saying when they were pointing at Jack and me and laughing—and after we had our passports stamped, we went out into the waiting area to look for the Teen Study in Paris people (part of the thing they promise parents is that they'll pick us up at train stations and airports).

"Do you see anyone who looks French?" Holly asked me, which was kind of a silly question because we were *in* France, but I knew what she meant. The waiting area was busy even at ten at night. Kids ran around, people wandered all over, voices yakked away in all sorts of languages, and everywhere there were signs in French.

We stood together for a minute; then I spotted a dark-haired hottie in a red gauze shirt who was holding a piece of cardboard with *Teen Study in Paris* written on it. "Hoo! A real live French hottie!" I said, forgetting for just a tiny fraction of a nanosecond that I was a GF to a really hot *über*fabu Mr. Yummy of my own.

"Where?" Holly asked, her head whipping around (evidently she forgot about Ruariadh for a minute, too).

"There! And he's ours!" I said, grabbing her arm with one hand, and Jack's carrier and the bags with the other one. "Come on, let's go check him out!"

Holly beat me to the hottie, but only because I've discovered that motherhood slows you down.

"Hello, I'm Holly Lester," I heard her say as I dragged my stuff over toward them.

"I am very pleased to meet you," the hottie said, giving her a five-star smile. He was black, tall, and majorly cute, not that I noticed. "I am Pascal Gachet—my mother is the director of Teen Study in Paris." He turned his smile to me. "And you must be . . . eh . . ."

I looked down to where he was staring at Jack in his carrier. I sighed an inner sigh of the extremely martyred (I really should get a sainthood for all the stuff I have to go through!), set Jack down, and held out my hand. "Hi, I'm Emily. Emily Williams. This is Jack. He's not real, so don't go all freaky on me or anything, but due to a circumstance totally out of my control with a teacher who hates my guts, I'm stuck having him with me while I'm here."

Pascal looked a bit stunned around the eyes (big, brown eyes that were almost as puppy-dog as Fang's), but kept his smile. "It is a pleasure to meet you as well. Olivier went to buy some cigarettes, but he will be back in a few minutes, then we can take you to the hotel."

"Olivier?" I asked.

"He's one of the instructors." Pascal gave Jack another odd look before we headed out toward a sign that said *Metro,* stopping by a newsstand to pick up the ciggy-smoking instructor (guy check: about six feet, blond, with swirly, almost curly hair, probably in his thirties, goatee, two earrings—cute, but a bit old); then off we went. I know you're wondering what Paris looks like, but I can't tell you. We ended up taking the subway—called the Metro here—out to the area in the sixteenth *arrondissement*, where the French-study people had their house.

(Side note: *arrondissement* is French for . . . uh . . . well, OK, I don't know what it's French for, but the whole city is divided into numbered sections, called *arrondissement*. The numbers get bigger the farther you are away from the center of Paris.)

The building wasn't really a *house* house; it was called a student hotel. The brochure Mom had said the building was three seventeenth-century houses smooshed together, but it didn't look like it was about to fall down or anything. It was pretty nice-looking. There were dorm rooms on the upper three floors, and on the lower two were classrooms and common rooms.

"Blah blah blah blahblahblah blah," Madame Gachet said as she opened a door for Holly and me. OK, OK, that wasn't really what she said, but that's what it sounded like to me. She was speaking in French and I didn't understand a single, solitary word.

"*Excusez-moi vous,* but I didn't quite get that. Could you *repeatez-vous?*"

Madame (she told us we had to call her Madame) frowned at me, looking me over like I was a piece of toilet paper stuck to her shoe. She looked like an older, female version of Pascal, only she had a big ol' hairy mole on one cheek, and her eyes weren't nearly as scrummy as Pascal's. She already had given me a weird look when I explained about Jack. I figured she was going to be another one of those people who don't like anything the slightest bit different. "You are from the Gobottle School, yes?"

51

"Yes, but I'm American. I didn't learn any French until I came to England last fall, and then I spent the first semester pretending to speak French, so really I only started learning it a couple of months ago, but everyone is years ahead of me, so I'm not getting a whole lot out of the classes. That's why Brother thought it would be good if I came here and did a couple of intensive weeks."

"Brother?" she asked.

"Everyone calls my father Brother. It's a long story. You'll just have to trust me that you don't want to hear it. Anyway, Brother said that being in France should help me learn more, although I have to say that I'm not totally convinced. I mean, doesn't everyone speak English?"

Her frown got all frownier. "The purpose of this program is to improve your skills at speaking and reading French, and that is what you will do. We do not often take beginner students, but I am sure we will have no difficulty accommodating you. This is your room. You will share with Sabine and Sephora Potter. They are from Georgia."

I followed Holly into the room. I wasn't very hot on the idea of sharing it with two strange girls, but the room was pretty cool. It was done in shades of red and cream, and the beds weren't bunk beds, like they had at the camp you and I went to a couple of years ago. These beds were scattered around the room, each with a stool and a dresser next to it. The ceiling was angled all weird, probably because we were in the attic, but the view was great. We could see down into a tiny little courtyard, which had white metal tables and a matching white metal spiral staircase. Scattered around the courtyard were pots of red and pink flowers. It just *reeked* of Paris!

While I was looking around at our new digs, Madame said something in French. Holly explained after Madame left that breffy was at seven, and that we'd be tested right afterward to find out where we were, French-wise.

Holly and I claimed our beds and were arguing over whether or not Pascal was a seven or a nine on the hottie scale (I said seven; she said nine because he had nice eyes, but Fang has nice eyes and he's much more a nine than Pascal ever will be) when the two girls from Georgia came in. I almost dropped Jack (he was crying again) when I saw them. They were twins, but not just any sort of twins; they were identical twins; dressed alike, groomed alike— they probably had exactly the same DNA and finger- prints. They also had that white-blond hair and pale red skin that makes you think albino.

"Hey, y'all," they said in unison in heavy Southern twangs.

"You must be our new roomies. Ah'm Sabine," one of them said, then nudged her sister.

"Ah'm Sephora," the other said.

Honest to Pete, they were *identical* identical! There was no way to tell them apart. They were both wearing jeans and black T-shirts. They both had on the same ear- rings. Their hair (shoulder-length bobs) was exactly the same. I tell you, it was positively creepy how much they looked alike!

"I'm Holly," Holly said; then she pointed at me. "This is my best friend, Emily. She's from the States, too."

"Oooh, you have a baby!" Sephora squealed as she came around the dresser to see me. "How adorable! Is it a boy baby or a girl baby?"

"A baby?" Serena said. "You got to bring a baby hee-yuh?"

I held Jack up (carefully—you really do have to watch his head). "It's fake. I know, too weird, but I have this teacher, and she hates me, so I'm stuck with him. His name's Jack."

They squealed to a stop in front of me, sliding each other looks out of the corners of their eyes like they thought I was insane or something. Me! I'm the most normal person I know!

"Fake?" one of the girls said (I'd forgotten who was who by that point).

"It's part of a teen pregnancy–prevention program," Holly said, coming to sit next to me, which was really sweet considering the Georgia twins were still looking at me like *I* was the weird one. "Emily had to bring her baby with her, but I keep telling her it's not going to be as bad as she says it will be. I think it's rather fun."

"Fake?"

They seemed to be kind of stuck on that point. "Fake. It means not real," I said slowly, then did the whole show-ing-Jack's-back thing while I explained why I was stuck with him.

One of the girls—Sephora, I think—took a deep breath

like she was going to scream or something, then let it all out in a gushy, "That is the verruh coolest thing Ah've evuh seen! Ah just wish Ah had a baby doll, too. Beanie, isn't that the verruh coolest thing?"

"Yes," Sabine said. "It looks so real, too! And it cries!"

"Incessantly," I said, but with a teensy bit of pride. After all, no one else in the program had a baby with her. I started to see how Jack might be a bit of fun after all. "But he's a very good baby normally."

Right at that moment, as if on cue, Jack shut up. The girls squealed again and begged to hold him. Holly shot me a "told you so!" look while I was giving them Jack-holding instructions.

"Is this all the clothes he has?" one of the twins asked as she rocked him.

"Yeah, although I have reusable diapers. He only pees water, and the diapers don't take long to dry out."

They looked disappointed. "Ah was hopin' we might be able to dress him up," the nearest one said. "Y'all should get him cute things, as long as y'all are heeyuh in Paris."

"Baby clothes!" Holly said brightly. "That would be fun. You could get him a couple of stylish Parisian baby outfits, Em."

I gave her a look. "Are you kidding? Don't you remember the baby budget we did? Baby clothes are expensive."

"Not if y'all looked at the market," Sephora (I think it was her) said. "We were theyuh this morning. It's called *le marché aux puces de Saint-Ouen*, and it's huge! Y'all will love it to bits."

"The Puces of Paris!" Holly said, all excited-like. "I've heard of that. It's a giant flea market, Emily. Oh, we should go! I'm dying to get a sexy French outfit, something that will make me look all wicked and temptressy."

See what I mean about her? She never wanted to be a wicked temptress before she met Ruariadh.

"I suppose we could go," I said with a yawn. "We have time tomorrow morning, right? After we do some test or other?"

"Only afternoons are free," Sabine said. Oh, all right, I have no idea if it was Sabine or Sephora, but I'm just going to guess from here on out. They're practically the same person; it really can't matter too much which is which, right? Right.

"We'd be happy to go with y'all to the market, if ya like," Sephora added.

We decided to go right after lunch. I figured it would be a good introduction to Paris, and who knew what I'd find? Maybe I'd see something that would drive Devon into a crazed frenzy, not that I'm sure that would be a good thing. It sounds like it would, but you know, after all my experience with Aidan and Ruaraidh, I've learned that what sounds good isn't necessarily good in person.

Anyway, I pried Jack from the twins' grips.

"He's just so darned cute," they gushed as I stuffed him into his carrier and set it next to my bed. "He's so perfect! He's just a doll!"

They laughed hysterically at their little joke.

"Oh, yeah, he's a doll all right," I said as I rolled my eyes. Honestly! You'd think they'd never seen a fake baby before!

I crashed then, not having gotten too much sleep because of Jack and my smoky room and everything.

Three hours later the twins weren't saying Jack was a doll. They were yelling at me for his waking everyone up. I dragged him out to the hall and sat in the bathroom for twenty minutes until he went back to sleep. He woke everyone up again a few hours later, so I ended up sleeping on the couch in the lounge.

This morning when I got up . . . Oh, poop, have to go. They're done testing everyone and we're going to get our class assignments. I'll be back as soon as I can.

Tell me what's going on with you guys. I miss you all, especially now that I'm in a foreign country. Well, OK, England was kind of foreign, but not really because I'm used to it, but France is *really* foreign!

Hugs and kisses,
~Em

Subject: Re: I'm here
From: EmInParis@parisstudy.com
To: DevTheMan@britnet.co.uk
Date: 10 April 2004 4:08 pm

DevTheMan wrote:

> glad you made it there safely, but that's a real pisser
> about having to take Jack with you. Don't suppose you
> can pull its battery pack or whatever?

I wish I could, but no, it's all sealed up, and if you try to break into the back of the doll, it registers that and *bzzt!* Immediate failing grade.

So how is the fishing thing with your dad going? Are you looking forward to coming to Paris and getting away from stinky fish stuff? I can't wait for you to come. I can't wait for my birthday! Oh. Geez. That sounds really pushy of me, doesn't it? Ignore that. I'm not being pushy. I mean, if you don't want to . . . *you know* . . . we don't have to. I'm sure we can do something else. Cards, maybe. Or there's French TV; it's kind of fun. You can tell me what the people are saying. Or we could go see a movie.

Oh, never mind. Just forget that I e-mailed you and mentioned doing it, 'K?

Big hugsy kisses,
Emily

Subject: Re: You really don't have to if I make you want to barf or something
From: EmInParis@parisstudy.com
To: DevTheMan@britnet.co.uk
Date: 10 April 2004 4:15 pm

DevTheMan wrote:
> *be silly, I've told you a hundred times that I want to.*
> *You're the only bird I've ever dated who thought I*
> didn't *want to. I do, OK? Comprendez-vous?*

You're mad at me, aren't you? You're mad and speaking snide French at me because you think I'm acting like a big baby, right? Well, I can't help it! I've never done this before! You have to cut me a little slack here, 'cause I don't know what I'm doing! Well, I mean, I *know*—I've seen the movies and had the talks, and besides, I watch HBO, so I know what happens—but I don't have any *practical* experience at it, and now you're mad at me because I wish I had!

I'm going to go sit on my bed and cry great big buckets of tears now. Just as soon as I've fed Jack.

Weepily,

Emily

Subject: Re: My heart, it is broken. Speaking like Yoda, I am.
From: EmInParis@parisstudy.com
To: DevTheMan@britnet.co.uk
Date: 10 April 2004 4:18 pm

DevTheMan wrote:
> *Emily, I swear to God above, I WANT YOU! I'm not*
> *mad, and I know you're scared, but I want you to stop*
> *thinking that I don't want you, because I do. A lot.*
> *OK? You're my girl, so stop worrying.*

Scared? *Moi?* Hahahahahah, I laugh! Concerned, yes. Curious, oh, yeah. Worried . . . mmm . . . OK. But scared? Bwahahahah!

Emily the *so* not scared

Subject: Re: Everything's OK in the girl department, right?
From: EmInParis@parisstudy.com
To: DevTheMan@britnet.co.uk
Date: 10 April 2004 4:20 pm

> *good. There's nothing to be scared about. It'll be fun.*
> *Erm . . . maybe not the first time, though. You're not*
> *one of those people who runs to the doctor for every-*
> *thing, are you? My sister had to go to hospital after she*
> *shagged her boyfriend because she thought she might*

> have picked up a disease from him. She fainted when
> they did a blood test.

OMG! *OMG!* TMI, TMI!

Emily the changing her mind about the whole thing . . .

Subject: Re: How do you find hotties wherever you
go?
From: EmInParis@parisstudy.com
To: Dru@seattlegrrl.com
Date: 10 April 2004 4:27 pm

Dru wrote:
> *understand it, I go places! I see things! But wherever*
> *you go, you find hotties. It's just not fair, especially*
> *since you have a BF. And a French hottie! Did he have*
> *an accent? Was it droolworthy?*

Pascal? Yeah, he has a French accent, and it is kind of
nice, but you know, it's not like I'm a hottie magnet or
anything. I'm going with Devon, so I'm not looking for
guys, and I can't help it if there are just oodles more
hotties in England and France than there are back home.
And I can't help but be polite to Pascal—Brother's always
on about being a good American and all that stuff—so
when Pascal stopped by my solitary-confinement room
this morning to see how I was doing, I forced myself to

chat with him. You're not buying that "forced" bit, are you? Sigh. I figured you wouldn't. You know me too well. OK, the truth is he's just absolutely scrumdillyicious, although I am not interested in him that way. He's just a friend. A really hot, nummy-eyed, drool-makingly fabu, *über*-hottie friend, but still just a friend.

Mmmrrowr!

> *I'm sorry you got stuck with Jack. That doesn't seem*
> *fair that everyone should have their babies for just*
> *three days, and you get stuck with yours for more than*
> *two weeks. However, I think you should listen to Holly.*
> *You could have fun with a fake baby! And I love the*
> *idea of buying him baby clothes! Have you seen them?*
> *Some of that stuff is so cute!*

OMG! I went shopping this afternoon with Holly and the y'all sisters, and you would not believe the cute things I bought for Jack! This Puces Market place is utterly fabu! It's actually a whole bunch of markets together, each with different sorts of stuff. There's an antique market (interesting but very pricey), furniture, shoes, plates and stuff, clothing—everything you can think of. Some of it is inside buildings; other parts of it are in the streets. It's very cool, but very crowded, and no one spoke English, so I had to stick tight to Holly and let her do the talking for me.

Anyhoodles, I got Jack four new outfits. They're used, but that's OK because A) he's fake, and B) the unused baby clothes are way too expensive. The cutest outfit I put on him right away (which, let me tell you, got me a few weird looks from the lady manning the used-baby-clothes booth when she saw the spot for the key in Jack's back). It's a ladybug romper! It's so cute—the top part is a green vest, and the bottom is red with big black lady-bug spots. It's so adorable! I also bought him a blue outfit with a big pink rat on the front that says in French, "Will you be my friend?" At least I think that's what it says. It could be something else, but there's definitely a "Will you" question in there somewhere.

I also got him an adorable dark blue Nehru jacket, and a sparkly green outfit that says Total Star on it, for evening wear.

We spent so much time shopping for Jack, no one got anything else, but it was a lot of fun, and S&S were actually pretty nice. They wanted to buy Jack stuff, too, but I said no. I didn't think it was quite right that they spend money on a doll I have to give back in two weeks.

Besides, the clothes I bought him were much cuter than what they picked out.

Oh, oh, oh! I also got a used baby backpack, so now I don't have to lug his baby carrier everywhere. Coolio, eh?

> Not much is happening here. Rachel barfed in history
> when she ate five Cadbury eggs for breakfast. Sukey
> got a wart on her toe, and cut it off rather than using
> that wart stuff. Her foot got infected and her mom
> took her to the emergency room (she had blood

> poisoning), but now she's better. OH! I totally forgot
> to tell you! I'm going to change my name! Dru is, like,
> so yesterday. I was thinking of changing it to
> Guinevere, because you know how I love her, but then
> I thought that might be too long. Then I thought Raven
> would be cool, but you really have to be dark-haired
> to be a Raven. So then I was thinking of using a belly-
> dancing name. Something cool and exotic. What do
> you think of Melantha?

Ooooh! I want to change my name, too! I've got an old-fashioned name; I want an *über*cool new name! I love Melantha, although I'm not sure you're the Melantha type. It sounds dark, too, and you're blonder than I am.

You have to help me think of a new name. That's the best idea you've ever had!

> forgot to tell me what happened with the Georgia
> peaches when Jack woke them up.

Well, good and bad happened. The bad was that they were peeved at me last night (although they mellowed out later, when we went shopping). The really bad was that Madame called me in and told me that she'd had complaints about Jack. Like I didn't know who complained?

"I must ask that you turn your doll off at night," Madame said to me after she hauled me into her office, a small little room off the main floor. "I realize that the doll is part of a school project, but I cannot have the other students disturbed every night."

"Trust me, if I could turn Jack off, I would! But I can't." I explained the whole horrible situation again. (I've found that with Brother you sometimes have to repeat yourself, so I figure it's the same with other old people—they just don't get it the first time.) "I'm sure you don't want me to fail the class and not get into Harvard because a couple of people can't wear earplugs, like I suggested they did before we went to bed."

"That is not the point," she argued.

"I'm not turning him off. I can't! It's impossible!" I explained again.

She got a bit nasty with me, saying things like I was going to cause trouble and stuff, so I ended up calling Brother and made him talk to her while I went out and had some juice and toast.

By the time I was done, evidently Brother had made her understand just how important the whole situation with my grades was, because she marched over to me and informed me (in a really snotty tone) that she was having my things moved to a private room.

"We do not normally do this, you understand," she said loud enough so that everyone in the dining room could hear her. Why is it people always insist on making me the center of attention? It's not like I want everyone staring at me! "It does not foster the spirit of friendship that we at Teen Study in Paris encourage, but upon the request of your father, I will make an exception. I am having a bed moved into an unused room for you. It is very small. You will share the bath with those in your *assigned* room."

"Thank you," I said politely, which is definitely bonus points for Emily because I really wanted to be snarky right back at her. I decided to shoot for mega extra bonus points. "I appreciate it."

She made a short little nod, then told me to be sure to report to the study room to take the French test.

Whoops, gotta run. We're going to the Eiffel Tower tonight on a group trip. I have a lot more to tell you! Paris is *über*ly cool!

Hugs and French kisses (NOT! Ahahahah!),
~Victoria . . . no, Serephina . . . Angharad? Poop. Just Em until I can think of something else.

Subject: My life in prison and the horrible attack by a warden
From: EmInParis@parisstudy.com
To: Dru@seattlegrrl.com
Date: 10 April 2004 11:33 pm

Dru wrote:
> *have to send me pictures of Jack in his ladybug*
> *outfit. It sounds too utterly cute! And no, I'm not*
> *buying any of that Little Miss Innocent biz with Pascal.*
> *You are so a hottie magnet! You've had three*
> *boyfriends since you left here!*

OK, first of all, I had one BF before Devon, and he turned out to be a major poophead, so he doesn't count. Ruaraidh was never mine. Well, he was, kind of, but he doesn't count either. So really Devon is my first English BF. And Pascal is just a guy, you know? Besides, it's OK to look. Eye candy, that's what Pascal is. Did I tell you he has *both* ears pierced? With tiny little gold hoops. *happy sigh*

I wonder if Devon has thought about getting his ears pierced?

> Solitary confinement? What do you mean, solitary
> confinement? I thought the director woman had
> calmed down about the Jack thing?

Yes, I mean solitary confinement—you know, just me all by my lonesome. What happened is this: I failed the French placement test. Madame said no one had ever failed it before, but I did. She said that it is supposed to test your knowledge of French, so they know which level of class to stick you in. Well, I took it and failed. Yeah, I know, it was kind of weird failing a test that was unfailable, but in the end, Madame said I was what she would classify as a prebeginner, so I had to be stuck in a class by myself.

Which actually isn't that bad, considering! I don't have a teacher watching over me all the time, I get to study whatever I want, and Jack doesn't bother anyone. Madame told me I could use the library as my study room while everyone else was in the classrooms, which is doubly cool, since I decided that my project for the two weeks of study was going to be reading a Paris *Vogue* rather than just looking at the cool pics. And hey, the computers are in the library. Can we say Internet fun? I think we can! I'm going to make Pascal an *Emily's Hottie of the Week* just as soon as I get a picture of him. (BTW, my HOTW site got listed on a search engine without me even trying! How cool is that?)

Anyhoo, that's why I'm in solitary confinement. The French part of the day is only three hours, so it's not too bad. Oh, you asked what my schedule is like. Here it is:

8:00 Breakfast (not the greatest, but not terribly gacky, either. Frankly, I expected like lots of French food—I mean, come on, I'm in Paris! Where's the French toast?—but there was just basically croissants and hard rolls, and hot chocolate, tea, or coffee).

9:00 French class (with a potty break from 11:00 to 11:15).

12:00 Lunch (much better food than breffy—lots of good bread and cheese and stuff).

14:00 Excursion A or B. This is optional—every day they take a group of students to two different places. We don't have to go, but some of things look kind of fun.

14:00 Sports and other activities for people who don't want to go on the sightseeing tours.

20:00 Dinner. (aka eight at night. Yes, eight! These French eat late. No wonder they're so cool.)

21:00 Evening activities (which includes games, something they call a cine-club (movies), and get this! Disco parties! DISCO!!!).

24:00 Check-in. (We have to be back by midnight, which is just a stupid, stupid rule. Who wants to spend their whole vacation in Paris being back by midnight? Even Brother lets me stay out later than midnight!)

So! Let me tell you about Day One: Emily Does Paris. After the French test, everyone was called together in the dining room and Madame introduced the teachers. There are three of them, and for the most part they seem to be OK, but *one* of them failed the Jack test.

What's the Jack test? Well, I've decided that since I'm stuck with Jack, and you and Holly and everyone else thinks he's kind of cool, and it really would be stupid for me to mope around all the time just because I'm suffering the curse of Horseface Naylor, I'd better make the best of it and deal. So I am. In the process of dealing I discovered that Jack makes a great test to see whether or not I'll like people. Pascal, the first Jack testee in Paris, liked him. So did the S twins (although they didn't like him during the night). Madame didn't like him. Snickerer Bee (who came in last night by train) rolled her eyes and said, "Why did you bring *that?* Are you delusional or something?"

See? Comprehensive scientific testing at its best! Any-hoodles, here for your reading pleasure are the official results of the Jack test.

Test subject: Delphine Fore
Teaches: Advanced French
Description: Mom-ish, but very New Age. Wears an amethyst crystal around her neck, and talks a lot about feng shui (whatever that is).
Jack test result: "Isn't that cute? What a very good way for young people to learn about the responsibilities of parenthood. That romper is *très bon, très chic!*"

Test subject: Mounia Zobel
Teaches: Intermediate French
Description: She's half-German, and could possibly be a Nazi. All I know is that she doesn't like me *or* Jack, and only a Nazi couldn't like a fake baby dressed in an *über*ly cute ladybug outfit.
Jack test result: Didn't say anything, just thinned her lips at Jack and me both. Bet she has a tattoo of I *heart* Hitler on her butt.

Test subject: Olivier Saville
Teaches: Beginning French, so technically I'm in his class, although he only came by the library twice today, so I'm hoping I don't have to see too much of him. On the bonus side, he is kind of cute in an older-man sort of

way, but on the deficit side, he's a smoker, which is just gross.

Jack test result: While he was talking to me in the library about what I wanted to do during my solitary confinement, he smiled at Jack and patted him on his head. Then he patted my shoulder like he was being all sympathetic when I told him about how I got stuck with Jack, and when I stood up to go to the magazine rack, his hand slid down my back and onto my butt! Yes! A butt fondle by a cigarette-smoking, really older man! Is that an ew cubed, or what!?!

Now you know me, I'm not rude or anything, but there's no way I was going to stand for a butt fondle. That is harassment, pure and simple, and I am *not* going to be a fondlee for anyone unless I like them enough to fondle them back, and the thought of that—old butt fondle? EW EW EW! So I made sure I stomped on his foot really hard as I walked by.

"Oh. Sorry," I said, smiling to myself when he did a funny little one-footed hop. "Didn't see you there. I'll just use this issue of Paris *Vogue* as my study text, OK? Oh, gee, is that the time? I have to call my father. He's a really important . . . uh . . . international detective guy in the police who throws pervy pedophiles and guys who hit on young girls into jail. He wanted me to call and tell him all about the school here. Yes, sirree, I'll just go call him now, and then when I'm done I'll do the vocabulary drill for you, 'K?"

"That would be fine, Emily," Olivier said in a strangled

voice. "Do not forget to listen to the lesson one dictation tape as well. I will . . . er . . . check back with you in an hour or so, yes?"

"Dine and fandy," I said brightly. "I should be through with my detailed, extensive call to my very important police father by then."

He gave me a watery smile and limped out to the classroom. I spent the rest of the morning watching a stupid "Learn French" videotape that was boring except for a fake soap opera. I didn't understand what was going on in it, but it was still fun.

Right after that was when Pascal came in to check on me. We chatted for a couple of minutes about the plans for the afternoon (trip to the Eiffel Tower); then he asked why I was in the library all by myself. I explained about the whole failing-the-test thing, and he laughed.

"You'll do well on your own. I will stop by to see you often."

"Oh, good," I said, trying to sound like I was a GF to a really hot BF and thus not interested in him in a BF sort of way, yet still appreciative of the fact that he was majorly droolworthy. "Maybe you can help me. Olivier said he thought it would be best if I learned something called survival French rather than Paris *Vogue* French, and since this videotape doesn't seem to have survival French lessons on it, I'm not quite sure what I'm supposed to be studying."

"Ah, that's just another way for saying the basic French you need to get around Paris," Pascal said with another five-star smile. "I will be happy to help you, if you like."

So he gave me a couple of phrases that I wrote down, and made me say them until I had the pronunciation right. And I figured that since you don't know any French, and you're my BFF, you have to share my pain and learn one a day, too. So here you go, here's the first Emily's Very Cool French Phrase for People Who Don't Speak French Well (EVCFPPWDSFW for short, although that's not very short, is it? Maybe I'll just call it Very Cool French and leave it at that):

Occupe-toi de tes oignons. This literally translates into "occupy yourself with your onions," but it means mind your own business.

"Really? Onions?" I asked Pascal when he told me that phrase.

"Yes. It is good to say when someone . . . eh . . . gets too close to you."

"Too close? Oh, you mean like if someone does a butt fondle. Yeah. Handy phrase, that," I said, thinking that I would be trying it out on Olivier if he thought he was going to grab cheek again. I looked down at my survival French phrases that I'd written down. "OK, so I say *bonjour* whenever I go into a shop, 'cause otherwise you're being impolite, and the metro is called *trom*é . . . um . . . I can't remember why."

"Verlan," Pascal said, pointing to a note I had made.

"Oh, that's right. It's like pig latin, where you reverse the syllables. Gotcha. I think I've got the hang of this survival French stuff! Very cool!"

"Très looc," he corrected. *"Looc* is verlan for cool."

"Right. And *bonjour* in verlan is—"

"Jourbon!"

"Coolio! I mean, oilooc!"

He laughed again and told me I would do fine.

You think that's weird? Get this—when we were at the Eiffel Tower (which is not nearly as big as I thought it would be, but still, the elevator ride up is fun and you do get to see a lot of Paris from the top), as we were standing on the observation deck, Sabine said, *"Oh, la vache!"*

I looked at Holly, who was standing as far back from the railing as she could get and still be on the Eiffel Tower (she has a thing about heights). "What did she say?" I asked in a whisper.

Holly whispered back, "She said, *'the cow'!*"

I gave her the eyebrow of inquiry. She pinched my arm. "You know, it's like saying 'holy cow,' or 'wow,' or an exclamation like that. Honestly, Emily, I don't know how you could have gone through two semesters of French and not learned about things like *oh, la vache.*"

"Yeah, well, I didn't start learning French in the womb like you English do. You're serious, though? It means *the cow*?"

"Yes," she said, her eyes closed tight so she wouldn't inadvertently look down and end up ralphing up her guts.

"Oh, come on, you can look out at the distance. You can't see the ground from here."

She peeled her eyes open and looked. "I suppose the Arc de Triomphe is pretty."

I nodded. I have to admit that the view from the Tour Eiffel (that's what they call it here, and no, it's not part of that verlan stuff) is slicker than snot on a doorknob, but the thing that surprised me was just how big Paris is! As far as you can see there are buildings, buildings, buildings, most of them in white or gray stone. No big skyscrapers, but lots of really old, fancy buildings. The Arc de Triomphe is this big arch thingy in the middle of a big flat area where a whole bunch of streets intersect. Snaking through the sea of buildings are little canals that are really streets, some of which look green because they are lined with trees. On the other sides of the Eiffel Tower you can see the Seine (that's the river that runs through Paris), and the Palais de Chaillot (pretty), and other palaces, and big parks, and stuff. It was all so . . . French!

"The cow, look at that," I said, pointing up through a grille. "It's the top of the Eiffel Tower. Coolio!"

"There's a cow on the top?" Sabine asked, looking around. "Where?"

"No, I said 'the cow' the way you say 'oh, la vache,' " I explained. "It means the same thing, I just said it in English."

"But we're in France," Sabine said, frowning.

Holly pretended to cough so Sabine wouldn't notice that she was giggling.

"Never mind," I said, going over to look down through the crisscross grille they put up to keep people from throwing themselves off. Sephora was looking down.

"What do you think would happen if y'all was to throw a penny down?" she asked.

I looked down. "Um . . . I've never thought about it."

"I bet if you threw a penny down and it hit someone on the head, you'd kill them," she said with a really creepy smile. "I bet it would split theyuh head right open just like a ripe ol' melon."

"A penny?" I asked.

"Yayus. It's because we're up so high. My daddy told me that if you toss a penny from this height, it would kill anyone it hit." She started rustling through her fanny pack. "Let's try it!"

"Um . . ." I edged away from her. There was just something too gruesome about the thought of splitting open someone's head with a penny. "I think I'll pass. My father is really big on the whole good-American-abroad thing, and I'm just willing to bet you that murdering people in the country you're visiting doesn't count as being a good American."

"Oh, come on; it'll be fun," she said.

Sabine strolled over to us. "Whatcha'll doing?"

"We're going to throw pennies and see what happens to them," Sephora said, holding out a handful of copper pennies (the French have three pennies—one cent, two cents, and five cents).

"Ooooh," squealed Sabine. "Daddy said if we threw a penny off the top, it would hit the pavement so hard, it would cut right through it like it was made of butter!"

"He did not; he said if it was to hit someone on the head, it could slice them open like a ripe melon," Sephora argued.

"Daddy wouldn't say thayat," Sabine drawled.

"Don't you tell me what Daddy would say; I was right there when he said it."

"You're not the only one he talks to," Sabine snapped.

I left the two of them arguing and toddled over to where Delphine was pointing out the sights to S-Bee and some others. I tugged on her sleeve until she stepped away from them. "Unless you want to be explaining to the French police why there are a whole bunch of people lying dead beneath the Eiffel Tower with their heads split open like ripe melons, you might want to tell Sabine and Sephora not to throw pennies off the deck."

"*Sacre!*" she said (I think it's like swearing lite), and hurried off to where the Bloodthirsty Twins were getting ready to fling pennies through the grille.

"There you are! Come on; I want to see the wax figures," Holly said, dragging me over to a glass case thingy that had two guys sitting around a table. One was supposed to be Thomas Edison; the other was Monsieur Alexandre-Gustave Eiffel (yes, there really was a Mr. Eiffel!). She posed next to the figures while I took her picture. "Isn't this thrilling? Oh, I wish Ruaraidh were here. He'd love to see Paris from the Tour Eiffel. I miss him so much!"

"Yeah, I know," I said. OHMIGOD! I'd forgotten about Devon! For the whole day, I hadn't once thought of him!

Well, except about wondering if he'd like his ears pierced. Still, that's not really *thinking* about him. It's not *missing* him.

Holly gave me a sympathetic look. "Poor Emily. I know you must miss Devon something terrible, too."

"Yeah," I said again, starting to feel really bad because the truth was, I hadn't missed Devon at all. I turned away from her and went to look at a barge that was going down the Seine.

"Em? I'm sorry, I didn't mean to upset you. Devon will be here in a week."

I did a shoulder shrug thing that I'd seen Pascal do (the French are really good shruggers). I'm a bad girlfriend. BAD!

"It's harder for you because I know I'm not going to see Ruaraidh except on breaks, but you're used to being with Devon whenever you want. Poor, poor Emily."

"Um," I said, feeling horrible and rotten inside. I bet you Devon thought of me today, at least once. I bet he missed me.

Sniffle.

"Em? You look funny. What's wrong? Are you feeling bad about Devon?"

I couldn't stand it any longer. "It's not like I don't want to not miss him," I said, whirling around to face her. "It's not like that at all. It's just that I haven't had the time to miss him today. First I had Madame on my case because of Jack; then there was the test, and the class, and octopus-hands Olivier, and Pascal, and then we had lunch and the bus tour around Paris, and then we were dumped off here, so when was I supposed to find time to miss him, huh? HUH?"

"Oh," Holly said. Just "oh." She looked at me weird, though.

"I know what you're thinking," I said, shaking my finger at her. "You're thinking I'm a bad girlfriend. You're thinking that a good girlfriend would miss her boyfriend when they were separated, right? You're thinking I don't love Devon enough! You're thinking that's why he doesn't want to do it with me, because there's something wrong with me, and what's wrong is that I don't love him enough to be missing him every bloody second of the day like you miss Ruaraidh! That's what you're thinking, isn't it? ISN'T IT?"

"No," Holly said slowly, her eyes big like she was shocked. "I wasn't thinking that at all."

That's what she said, but I knew the truth—Devon doesn't want me anymore because I'm A) ugly when I'm naked, and B) not as in love with him as I should be.

I'm a horrible girlfriend. I should turn in my GF card right here and now.

Sniffle, sniffle, sniffle.

I was too bummed to enjoy the dinner we had at the Le Jules Verne restaurant on the second floor of the Eiffel Tower, even though it was a really elegant restaurant, and everyone there thought Jack was too cute (I put him in his Nehru jacket for the evening out).

I'm going to bed. I'm too depressed to tell you any more, not that there is much more to tell.

Sad and depressed hugs and kisses,
~Em

Subject: Sniffle
From: EmInParis@parisstudy.com
To: DevTheMan@britnet.co.uk
Date: 10 April 2004 11:35 pm

If you don't want me to be your girlfriend anymore, I'll understand.
   Emily

Subject: Re: Will you stop already!
From: EmInParis@parisstudy.com
To: Dru@seattlegrrl.com
Date: 11 April 2004 8:40 am

Dru wrote:
> *Cheese in a basket, girl! You're the only person I know*
> *who could go to Paris and work herself up into a hissy*
> *fit over nothing! You're not a bad girlfriend. You're*
> *not ugly naked! Devon does too want to do it with*
> *you! Will you stop with the pity party already?*

Geesh, you're supposed to be my friend and support me in my time of great need, not lecture me like Holly did last night. Oh, all right, I feel better. I was pretty depressed when I went to bed, but this morning I decided that I was just PMS-y or something. I do miss Devon; it's just that what with being in a foreign country and learning how to say things like *voulez-vous cesser de me cracher dessus pendant que vous parlez* ("will you stop spitting on me while you are speaking"—and yes, that's your phrase for the day), I just didn't have brain RAM to miss Devon, too. I think maybe I need to defrag my brain. Or upgrade to a bigger brain hard drive, heh heh heh.

>say "the cow"? You're kidding me, right?

Nope. They really do say it. So I'm going to, too—only not in French, because that's like, you know, so common.

> OMG, those twins are just too creepy! Did they kill
> anyone? I watched CNN this morning and they didn't
> say anything about people dying at the Eiffel Tour, so
> I guess they didn't?

It's Eiffel Tower or Tour Eiffel—you can't mix them up or people glare at you. And no, Delphine stopped them just as they were going to throw a couple of big euro coins over.

This morning the GTs (Gruesome Twins) stood up at breffy when Madame was asking what sites we'd like to see in the afternoon. She takes suggestions in the morning, and then we vote on what we'd like to see (although we don't have to go with the group—if Madame thinks we know enough French, we can go out on our own, which pretty much means I have to go with someone).

"I thought perhaps a visit to Notre Dame to hear a Gregorian chant of 'The Lament of Rachel' this evening would be enjoyable by all," Madame said. "Before we visit Notre Dame, we can take a walking tour of the Left Bank."

"Notre Dame?" Sabine asked. "That's a church? Could we visit the Bastille instead? We'd like to see where all those people were held prisoner before they were guillotined."

"Ooh, yes, the Bastille," Sephora said. "And then the Catacombs! All those dead bodies!"

"And Montfaucon, where they used to hang people," Sabine added.

"And the Place de la Concorde! I read about it before we came—that's where they guillotined a whole ton of people," Sephora said to Holly, who was sitting next to her. Holly looked like she was going to ralph up her croissant right then and there.

Madame clapped her hands in that old-people way that means she wants everyone to shut up. "We have several suggestions before us, but I would like to suggest that we leave the Catacombs for a day when Olivier can join us, as he is the expert on medieval history."

"The Bastille, then," Sabine said. "That sounds ever so much more interesting than a boring old church."

"Unfortunately, the Bastille is no longer in existence,

although there is a monument that commemorates the destruction of the prison, which was the beginning of the Revolution."

"Well, donkey dung," Sabine said disgustedly, sitting down and making a face at Madame when she wasn't looking.

"Notre Dame has gargoyles," I said, being Brother's daughter and thus having learned all sorts of boring medieval facts despite not wanting to know them. "Those are kind of scary. And it probably has a crypt; lots of those old churches did. There're dead people in a crypt."

"It's no Bastille," Sephora said with a matching pout. "I heard that one of the Bastille's wardens had his head cut off by a pocketknife."

"And later it was walked around the streets on a pike," Sabine said, nodding. "Now, that would be something to see!"

Holly jumped up and ran out of the room, her face as green as a frog. I pushed away my plate and tried not to think about how long it would take to cut off someone's head with a pocketknife.

Pascal grinned while Madame shot the GTs an evil look. "A discussion of the Revolution will be held next week, followed by a walking tour of the major sites of interest. Very well, the evening's outing is settled: Those of you who are at intermediate and above levels may go out on your own if you desire, while the beginners and those interested will take the walking tour, then attend the concert at Notre Dame."

"But that's not fayuh; we didn't vote," Sabine complained (she and Sephora are beginners in French, too). "I want to see something interesting! My daddy didn't pay for us to come all the way to Paris, France, just to see a church!"

Madame ignored her. I thought the chants sounded like torture, but when Holly got back from barfing up her breakfast, she looked so excited by the idea that I gave in and agreed to a walking tour and Notre Dame visit.

Gotta run. After we see the Left Bank and listen to the chants, I'm hoping we'll nab Pascal and hit a couple of Paris clubs! I'll let you know all about it later.

Oh, almost forgot—I love the name Sonora, but isn't that like some city name? Then again, one of my mom's cousins is named Philadelphia, so I guess there's nothing wrong with having a city name.

I'm thinking about something like Alexandrina. What do you think? Too long?

Hugs and kissies,
~Boring old Em

Subject: Re: Feeling a bit blue, are you?
From: EmInParis@parisstudy.com
To: DevTheMan@britnet.co.uk
Date: 11 April 2004 8:50 am

DevTheMan wrote:
> *homesick? If not, I'm sorry, I must have done*

> *something that made you mad at me, although I don't*
> *know what.*

You didn't do anything, Devon, except be your perfect funny, adorable self. It's me. I'm a bad girlfriend. I think you deserve someone better, someone who thinks about you every single minute of the day. Holly thinks about Ruaraidh like that.

Wah! I'm setting you free, Devon. Go off and have a really, really happy life. Without me.

Emily

Subject: Re: Now you're just being silly
From: EmInParis@parisstudy.com
To: DevTheMan@britnet.co.uk
Date: 11 April 2004 8:52 am

DevTheMan wrote:
> *I'm not Ruaraidh and you're not Holly, so stop*
> *comparing us to them. I like you the way you are, and*
> *wouldn't want you thinking about me every single*
> *minute of the day. You've got a brain, Em, and I like*
> *brainy birds. So stop saying you're a bad girlfriend*
> *and start planning what you're going to wear on your*
> *birthday. Make it something easy to take off, wink*
> *wink, nudge nudge.*

Oh, Devon! That's the sweetest thing you've ever said to me! Not the brainy bit, the part about making my clothes easy to take off.

I think I'm going to cry.

Emily

Subject: Re: Em? EM???
From: EmInParis@parisstudy.com
To: Dru@seattlegrrl.com
Date: 13 April 2004 11:09 am

Dru wrote:
> *It's been a whole day since I heard from you. Are you*
> *OK? You didn't get sick drinking the water, did you?*
> *E-mail me ASAP. You're starting to worry me!*

You are not going to believe what happened to us. In the middle of Paris. Twice. And then afterward . . . Wait, I have to do this right, one step at a time and all that crap.

I'm not sick, although Holly has another cold from our little "adventure." I couldn't e-mail you yesterday because almost the whole day was spent talking to Brother and Mom on the phone, and Madame and the police and everyone, and then Jack decided to have one of his bad days, so I was constantly feeding and changing him, and everyone who didn't know about him wanted to know why I had a realistic fake baby with me and *what* his problem was, and . . . Now, see, this is why I have to tell the story properly, 'cause otherwise it's just too confusing.

Here's the whole amazing thing in order of the events: After breakfast on Sunday Holly and I went to the Left Bank on a walking tour with Delphine and Mounia and a bunch of the other kids. The Left Bank is the coolio part of Paris, and has lots of really neat shops that Delphine and Mounia wouldn't let us stop at, but Holly and I decided that we'd come back another day and have a good old-fashioned shopping blowout.

We wandered around while D and M pointed out sights, stopping now and again to let us take pictures.

"What are y'all going to do tonight?" Sabine asked at one point during a photo stop. "I heard there's a place called the Assassin's Club that has terrible people in it. You know, terrorists and anarchists and those types. Sephy and I were thinking of getting a group together to see it. Y'all want to come with us?"

"Er . . ." I glanced over at Holly. Because Devon was coming over next week (which means we'd be doing romantic stuff together without Holly), I promised her that I wouldn't abandon her until then. Holly looked at me, making furious "I don't want to see assassins and terrorists and anarchists" eyebrows. "Thanks, but we have plans tonight."

"Really?" Sabine tipped her head to the side. "Whatcha'll doing?"

"The American Library," I said at the same time that Holly said, "Notre Dame."

Sabine looked disappointed. "Oh. Sounds dull either way you slice it."

I waited until she went off to see what her Gruesome Twin was doing (holding up a plastic shrunken head that she found in a cart outside a touristy shop) before tackling the subject at hand.

"How about we see if Pascal wants to take us out clubbing tonight?" I asked casually. "They have a Hard Rock Café here; I bet Pascal would like to go to that. You'd like it, too. We could dance, and take our pictures next to cool people, and fun stuff like that."

Holly frowned. We were walking down the Boul' Mich (Boulevard St. Michel, but only tourists call it that; if you're hip, you call it Boul' Mich), which is the student area of Paris. The Sorbonne is here, so it's a very cool area with lots of cafes and belly dancers and tiny little outdoor bookstores-in-a-cart.

"Oh, look, do you think those are *gamins* or child *clochards*?" Holly nodded toward a couple of kids swarming a lady in a white pantsuit. Pascal had warned us about the *gamins* (technically it means kids, but in this case it means the kid pickpockets who evidently are everywhere in Paris), and the *clochards* (bums).

"*Gamins,* definitely. What about the Hard Rock?"

Holly stopped in front of a gyro stand and made her worried face. "You don't want to go to Notre Dame with the rest of school? I thought it would be interesting to hear a Gregorian chant in person. They're very relaxing and good if you want to meditate. And, of course, they're historical. Your father would probably like to know you listened to an authentic French Gregorian chant at Notre Dame."

"Yeah, well, what turns Brother's crank is not necessarily what turns mine." I gestured toward the huge hordes of people squeezing down the busy sidewalks (it was a very touristy area). "We're in Paris, for heaven's sake, Holly! Exciting, thrilling Paris! On our own, with no parental units to cramp our style, and your idea of wild fun is a Gregorian chant?"

"It's cultural, and you said you were embracing other cultures," she said, wringing her hands.

"I already have; I've embraced two cultures—the English and now the French. Besides, embracing doesn't mean you have to go to churches. I mean, shoot, Holly, it's a church! Just a big old church with big old boring church singing!"

"You don't know that it will be boring," Holly said stubbornly. "You probably haven't ever heard Gregorian chanting before."

"Brother's dragged me to enough ancient churches; I can pretty much guarantee you that it'll be boring."

She did the hand-wring thing again. "This is a special church, though. They have statues of knights and things like that."

"I'm off guys dressed like knights unless they are named Devon or were in the *Lord of the Rings* movies."

"The gargoyles—you'd like them! We could have our pictures taken next to them. Wouldn't that be fun?"

I gave in. There would be lots more nights to see the clubs—Pascal told me the ones in the basements are called *caveaux*, or caves (how cool is that?)—so I let her talk me into seeing Notre Dame that night. "All right, we'll go if you're so interested in it. Hey, look at that—it's the street you saw in the guidebook."

Branching off to the left was a tiny little narrow street that Holly had read about. It wasn't much of a street, to tell you the truth—it was so narrow it looked more like an alley. On the corner of a cream stone building was a big brass sign that marked historical sites. Above it was a blue-and-white street sign that read *Rue du Chat-qui-Pêche*. Between the two, and all the way down the street, was a whole lot of graffiti.

" 'The street of the cat who fishes,' " Holly said in her breathless, tourist voice. "It's the shortest street in all of Paris—only thirty meters long." (That's about a hundred feet, BTW.) "The book said that it was named for a cat who took advantage of the Seine flooding the cellars of the houses to go fishing."

"Uh-huh, fascinating, thrilling, and absolutely astounding," I said, looking down it. There was a couple pressed up against one side of the narrow street, snogging for all they were worth. "I think I may just die right here on the spot, it's so exciting."

Holly whapped me on the arm as she started forward.

"Come on; let's take our pictures at the end of the street."

I looked over my shoulder. Delphine and Mounia and the rest were turning down the street that led to the Musée Cluny (it has the famous "Lady with the Unicorn" tapestry that your mom embroidered on her antique rocker). "OK, but just for a few minutes. I promised Bess I'd take a picture of the unicorn tapestry, and you know how obsessed she is with unicorns—if I don't get a close-up of it, she's threatened to shave off my eyebrows while I sleep."

Holly giggled. "Don't worry; I won't risk your eyebrows. We'll just run to the end, take our pictures next to the Seine, then catch up to the others."

We toddled past the couple snogging and stood at the end of the street taking turns with the camera. I was snapping a couple of shots of Holly posing when all of a sudden a huge herd of kids came out of nowhere. I mean, it was like they oozed out of the walls or something! One minute it was just Holly and me; the next we were surrounded by a swarm of kids.

"English? English?" they yelled, grabbing our arms and hands and all chattering in really fast French.

"Yes, we speak English," Holly said just seconds before she was swallowed up by a horde of raving kids.

"OHMIGOD, it's the *gamins*," I yelled, slapping a hand protectively over the zipper of my fanny pack, but someone's hand was already there. "EEK! *GAMINS!* Help, we're being attacked by *gamins!*"

I heard Holly shouting, but I was too busy beating the *gamins* off me and my fanny pack. Honest to Pete, Dru, they were everywhere! There were hands in my jeans pockets, hands in Jack's backpack, a ton of hands trying to jerk my fanny pack off me, more hands trying to get the digital camera . . . it was terrible!

"Police!" I screamed at the top of my lungs. "*GEN-DARME! Helpez-vous* us!"

Just like they had a switch or something to turn them off, the *gamins* jumped away from us and raced down the tiny street, laughing and jeering and probably saying all sorts of potty-mouth things in French to us. I staggered back against one of the graffiti walls and clutched at the camera. "Cheese on rye, that was awful. Are you all right?"

Holly was slumped against the railing that marked the end of the street, crying a little as she pulled her jacket on. The *gamins* had pulled it off her, trying to take it as well. Thank God I had Jack strapped into the backpack, because if I didn't, the *gamins* probably would have taken him, too. As it was they got Holly's purse (including her wallet and all her spending money), her bag with the sweater she'd just bought for her mom's birthday, and the digital camera case I had set down behind me. "Yes, I think so, but oh, Emily, they got my things! My bag and Mum's sweater! What am I going to do?"

"First off, we're going to find Delphine and Mounia and make them take us to the police so you can file charges against those *gamins*," I said grimly as I pulled her to her feet and helped her get her jacket on. "Then we're going to get the Thomas Cook people to replace your traveler's checks. You haven't changed much, have you?"

She shook her head, big tears rolling down her cheeks. "No, but they got Mum's Visa that she lent me. She's going to kill me!"

"No, she won't," I said firmly, mostly because you have to be firm when someone is crying after they have been attacked by *gamins,* but also because I was feeling a little like sitting right down and bawling myself. Those *gamins* were scary! They weren't very old—probably ten or twelve, some of them even younger—but the way they swarmed! And their hands were everywhere. Just thinking about it made me all shaky and stuff, but Holly was much more a victim than me, so I pushed the shaky feeling down and we set off after our school's group.

Fifteen minutes later we stopped outside a big white building. We'd been walking through narrow streets lined with tall white and gray buildings, climbing steadily. "Where are we?"

"Erm . . . we were on Rue Mouffetard . . . maybe this is Place Monge?" Holly said, turning around the map of Paris we'd been given. "The Cluny Museum should be around here somewhere."

I looked at the big building behind her. It had a huge dome, lots of steps, and a bunch of tall white columns. It could be a museum. "That looks like a museum. Why don't they post signs so people know where they are?"

Holly turned around and squinted at the building. "Oh, no."

"Oh, no, what?" I asked, taking a quick picture of it, because you never know when you might see something important.

"That's the Pantheon, not the Cluny. We're all turned about."

"Poop. Oh, Jack, not now . . ." Jack started crying. People standing around us at the street corner shot me odd glances until I pulled the backpack off. "Great, just what we need. You going to be OK if I take care of him?"

Holly nodded and followed as I went to sit down on the steps of the Pantheon. Just as I was feeding Jack his bottle, a short, dark-haired woman came up to us. "English?"

Holly whimpered and scooted over close to me. I glared at the woman, who looked like a bag person with skanky hair, a dirty shirt and pants, and an even dirtier coat. "You're way too old to be a *gamin*."

"You are English," she said again as she bared her teeth. They were horrible teeth, Dru, the sort of teeth they show in grade school to make little kids brush their teeth. This woman's teeth were all brown and yellow and icky. "I am from Romania. Give me money."

"The cow!" I said, getting to my feet so the street woman wasn't lurking over me. "First of all, I'm not English; I'm American. And second, I don't give a frog's bidet where you're from; I'm not giving you any money. My friend and I were just *gamin*ed, so even if we wanted to, we don't have any money to give. Just as soon as I'm finished feeding my fake baby, Jack, I'm taking my friend to the police, and if you don't want us to report you, too, you can just leave us alone."

"Give me money!" the woman said, grabbing Jack's leg.

"Hey, that's mine! Let go of him!"

The woman looked down at Jack in surprise for a moment as she realized that he wasn't real; then she bared those horrible teeth at me again and jerked Jack out of my hands. The key in his back kept her from getting him from me altogether, but for one horrible second I had visions of her running off with Jack, and me having to explain to Miss Horseface how I'd lost my Baby Annoy U in the middle of Paris. She wouldn't only fail me for the class, but she'd also make me pay for it, and those babies are *expensive!*

"Stop it! Give him back; you'll screw up my record!" I yelled, grabbing Jack's arm and pulling him back.

The woman hung on, saying something I didn't understand. Jack's arm made a horrible cracking sound.

"Let go of him; this is going to be recorded as abuse!" I couldn't jerk Jack too hard because it would show up that I shook him or something, but the woman wouldn't let go. She just kept saying stuff with those ghastly teeth, edging backward toward the road.

Behind me, Holly made that gulping noise that meant she was about to burst into tears, but she surprised me. She leaped to her feet and rattled off some really quick

French in a loud voice that had everyone walking by stopping to look. I jumped forward and stomped on the Jack-grabbing woman's foot. She howled and clawed at me, but I twisted out of her way, thankfully taking Jack with me, although his left arm hung all wonky.

I held him to me, quickly popping the bottle in his mouth so he would register that he was being fed, and clutched him to my chest while Holly stood up to the street woman, firing off what I gathered was really wicked French at her. A couple of people standing by nodded and added stuff of their own until the street woman spit on the sidewalk next to me, then turn around and stalked off.

I looked at Holly, all surprised and amazed and grateful. "Wow, Holly! Go, you!"

She thumbed her nose at the back of the street woman, then turned back to me, flushed with triumph. "I couldn't stand by while she stole Jack from you."

I gave her a quick hug, Jack and all. "That was amazing. You were so in her face! You rock, girl!"

She grinned and sat back down next to me as I finished feeding Jack his bottle of water. "I just did what I thought you would do if I were you."

I gave her a look from the corner of my eye. "Huh? Why would you want to do what I would do?"

"You refuse to be a victim," she said, her eyes kind of shiny, like she was really happy. "You don't let people push you around. I want to be like that, but I never thought I could do it until now. It's all because of you,

Em. You've shown me I can stand up and not let people make me feel bad."

I got a bit sniffly over the warm fuzzies, so I hugged her again, and we laughed over the woman's expression when Holly laid into her. By the time Jack was done, we were both through feeling woobidy over the *gamins,* and we went off to find the rest of the gang at the Cluny.

By the time we got there, they'd already left for the Notre Dame concert. I ran to the gallery that had the unicorn tapestry, pulled the camera out of my sweatshirt (I'd stuck it there to keep it safe, since I didn't have the case anymore), took a couple of pictures for Bess, and ran back out. We had to take the metro to the Notre Dame, since Holly's knee, which she'd wrenched fighting the gamins, was hurting a lot. But we got there (eventually), and made it over to the section of the church where everyone from our school was sitting.

"Where y'all been?" Sephora asked in a whisper as I slipped into a pew next to her. Holly collapsed on the other side of me, rubbing her knee. "What's wrong? You look horrible!"

"Thanks for that news," I said wryly. "We were *gamin*ed and *clochard*ed, and Holly lost her wallet and passport and money and the sweater she bought for her mom, and then we got lost and ended up at the Pantheon, where Holly was really brave and yelled at the *clochard* in French when she tried to steal Jack. After that we got on the wrong Metro, and had to get out at the next stop and walk back, but Holly's leg was hurting, so it took us a while to get back to it and get on the right Metro to take us here."

Sephora stared at us with her mouth hanging open. "Golly! All thayat in just a couple of hours? Next time you go sightseeing, I want to come with you. What did the pickpocket look like?"

People in the row behind us shushed us. I thought about telling them it was just a Gregorian chant, but remembered in time that I was a good American and it would probably be too rude to tell people that chants weren't really music; they were just words. Instead I leaned into Sephora and whispered, "It was a whole gang of them, gypsy *gamins*. The oldest was probably twelve. They stole Holly's stuff. We'll have to report them to the police after the concert."

She sucked in her breath in a simultaneously horrified and delighted sort of way. "I want to come with y'all when you do thayat. They might have a murderer or an arsonist or mugger at the police station. Wouldn't that be excitin'?"

"Yeah, real exciting," I said, doing the wry thing again. Honestly, Dru, the GTs were just too G for words!

We were shushed again, and Mounia, sitting on the other side of Sabine, gave me the eye, so we spent the next half hour listening to a bunch of guys do the Gregorian thing.

Since you haven't been to Notre Dame, I'll describe it for you: it's big. And gothic-y. You know, all cathedral-like, with great big stone arches and swoopy gothic ceilings, and stone pillars and stuff. It also has some pretty stained-glass windows, not the usual type that Brother likes, with scenes out of the Bible and saints and stuff, but round rose windows that look like really pretty kaleidoscopes. The shape of Notre Dame is kind of like a big T—at one end (the crossed part of the T) are the two big square towers above the main rose window. The long body of the the T is the rest of the cathedral, which is tall and narrow, and supported by flying buttresses (big arches that lean into the building and hold the walls up, and no, there are not butts on them, ahahahah). I have to say that as old churches go, it's pretty awesome, but I'm not really one for old churches. I was more worried about how we were going to get Holly's passport and wallet back than standing around oohing and aahing over the surroundings.

"I see you have decided to join us at last," Mounia said as soon as the chanting was over. She grabbed both me and Holly and dragged us over to a niche holding a saint or some other dead guy. "If you agree to accompany us on an excursion, it is considered polite to actually stay with the group. I realize that you do not care for the thoughts of others, but your selfish actions caused much concern when you disappeared earlier. Delphine hunted for you up and down the Boul' Mich, causing her to miss *entirely* the visit to the Musée Cluny."

"We're sorry," Holly said quickly, before I could tell Mounia that she could stick her Boul' Mich where the sun doesn't shine. "We only stepped away for a minute to take a quick picture, but then we were overcome by *gamins.*"

"*Gamins?*" Mounia said.

"Pickpockets," I explained. "A great big herd of them. They—"

Mounia snorted. "Were you not warned about carrying valuables with you?"

"Yes, but—"

"I thought so. You have no one to blame but yourselves if you *were* robbed," she said really snottily, like she didn't believe us. "People who are foolish enough to disregard Madame's warnings reap what they have sown. Paris is a safe city. The school's safety record is par excellence. Parisians themselves are polite and helpful. It is only the tourists who ignore the helpful advice of those who know the city well who fall victim to the itinerants and gypsies."

I ground my teeth. "Look, *we* are the victims here—"

Mounia flared her nostrils and interrupted me. *Rudely!* "I do not have time to debate the issue with you now. It is time for us to take the tour Madame has kindly arranged with one of the priests to show us all the historically important points of this most fabulous cathedral."

Holly plucked at my jacket sleeve.

I wanted to yell at Mounia, but dealing with impossible people—OK, most of them have been English, but still, they were impossible just the way Mounia is impossible—during the last six months has wised me up. Some. A little. Kind of. "You know what? I think we're going to pass on this fabulous tour of the fabulous cathedral, and instead take ourselves back to the fabulous home away from home. So knock yourself out with the tour, and we'll see you later."

Mounia snorted and turned toward the back of the church, where Delphine was gathering our group.

"Thank you, Emily," Holly said, breathing a sigh of relief. "I don't think I like her very much."

"News at five: I don't either."

"Have y'all been up to the tower to see the gah-goyles?" Sephora sidled up to ask. "We went earlier. No big whoop, *I* thought, but Beanie liked them."

"Only the truly ugly ones," Sabine said. "They looked, *you know*, satanic. Satanic! Right he-yah in a Catholic church!"

I scooted out of the pew, pulling Jack and his backpack around onto my back. It took me a minute to stop my inner chortle (Sabine's nickname was BEANIE! Have you *ever*?), but I managed to say (with a completely straight face, I'll have you know, and how easy is that when you have just found out the person you're speaking to is also known as Beanie?), "No, we were . . . uh . . . sidetracked and haven't seen anything here yet. Are the satanic gargoyles worth the climb? 'Cause I'd hate to go to all the trouble to climb to the top if they weren't really awful-looking. They're not Disney-ish satanic, right? They're not cutesy horrible?"

"Oh, no, they're truly repulsive," Sabine said. "Y'all have to see them, you just *have* to see them."

I glanced at Holly. "Well, I'm game if you are. How's your knee? Up to some stairs and repulsive gargoyles?"

Holly frowned toward the front of the church. "We told Mounia we were going back to the house."

"Mounia, schmounia, you know enough French to get us home later. I have to admit, I'm kind of curious about the gargoyles. It would be cool to get our pictures with them!"

"Very cool," Sabine said. "We'd go with you, but that priest who showed us all up there earlier said there was a sculpture of the slaughter of the innocents on the south side of the building, so we're going to see that."

Holly chewed her lip. "I wouldn't mind seeing the gargoyles, but I thought the sign said the tours were over? It's after seven. They have a rope across the door to the stairs."

"Oh, don't you worry none about thayat!" Sephora said, smooth as silk. "We'll just ask that there priest a question while you two slip behind him. No one will be the wiser."

I looked over to where Sephora was pointing. At the front of the church was a stone stairway in one of the towers. Across the stair was a red velvet rope on which hung a sign that probably read, *Closed*, in French. Across the entryway next to a table for donations and leaflets and stuff was a priest in a long black cassock. "I suppose we could."

"What if we get in trouble?" Holly whispered, her fingers doing the sleeve clutching thing again.

"Don't be silly; how could we get in trouble? We're just going to take pictures. It's not like we're going to vandalize the place."

"Trouble?" Sephora laughed. "Y'all won't get into trouble. There's nothing up theyuh but some stairs and a great big bell and the gargoyles. Go on; we'll ask the priest a couple of questions. Y'all go have a good time."

Holly pinched my arm as I started toward the entry area. "Remember what happened at Nethercote castle? You said all we would do was look at the dungeon and you got stuck in a medieval mantrap."

"That was an accident! Besides, it can't possibly happen here; there are no mantraps on these stairs."

"That's not what I mean, and you know it," Holly hissed, still tugging at my arm.

"Nothing is going to happen. Look, there's no door to the stairs, so we can't be locked into the tower, and they don't lock all of the doors to the cathedral at night because people come in to pray, so we'll be able to get out whenever we want. The worst thing that can happen is someone will see us up there, and if that happens and they yell at us, we'll just say we don't understand them, and leave. OK?"

"I don't like it—" she started to say.

"Consider it a broadening experience," I said, grabbing her hand. "Hurry, the GTs have that priest with his back to the stairs."

"GTs?" she asked as I ducked under the rope. It got

stuck on Jack, but Holly hurriedly destuck me before slipping under it herself.

"Gruesome Twins. Oh, good, they left the lights on." I started up the narrow stone staircase, Holly right behind me.

"They are kind of gruesome, aren't they? How high do you think this is?"

I trotted up the spiral stone stairs, one ear listening in case someone was coming down, the other waiting to hear a shout that meant the priest had noticed us. "Don't know, but you don't have to worry; I won't make you stand at the edge and look down. I know how heights make you woozy."

"They don't make me woozy," Holly protested.

I rolled my eyes at that, because she really is afraid of heights, but if she wanted to be brave Holly, who was I to tell her she wasn't?

The stairs seemed to go up and up and up. They were worn away in the center so that they almost looked bent. I was really grateful the lights were left on, because the walls looked like they were really thick (those medieval guys liked them that way), and the window slits that were supposed to let in light weren't very frequent. Plus it was dark out, so there was no light to be let in.

"Sheesh, I'm going to get a nosebleed if we go any higher," I panted as we went up even more. Holly didn't say anything, and when I looked behind me, her face was all pale like she was scared, and she had one hand clutching the wall. "Hey, if this is too much for you, I don't mind going up alone—"

"No, I'm fine. You came to the cathedral for me; I'll see the gargoyles for you."

I grinned. "You're getting pretty good at that brave stuff, you know."

After about a gazillion hours of climbing, we staggered through a wooden doorway and finally hit the top. Only it wasn't the top. It was just a floor with a gift shop, which was closed. An arrow pointed upward to another staircase.

"You OK?" I asked, after we panted and heaved and gasped and all that. "Want to stay here while I go on?"

"No. I'll come."

"I'll take your picture next to a gargoyle. Ruaraidh will like that, don't you think?"

She brightened up at that thought, and after gasping, etc., for a bit longer, we started up the second set of stairs. This one was smaller than the first, although just as spirally. It was darker, although there were still lights on, but the air was nastier. Close, Brother would call it, and I could see why. It smelled . . . old.

I looked back to see how Holly was. Her lips were tight, like she was holding back a scream. I wanted to get her to relax, and thought about joking with her, or talking about Ruaraidh, or something like that that would get her mind off the height thing, but to be honest, I just didn't have the breath. It's a LONG WAY UP those towers!

Suddenly we hit the top and burst out into open air.

"Oooh . . . gar . . . goyles!" I said, pointing as I doubled over to catch my breath. "Break . . . time!" I slid Jack's backpack off and leaned against the cold stone wall of the cathedral as I looked at the gargoyles. Holly stared in horror out at the lights of Paris that were twinkling away like mad, her fingers clutching each other so hard they were positively white in the dim yellow lamp that hung above our heads. "Don't look down; it'll just freak you out. Do you still have your guidebook? Why don't you read the bit about the gargoyles?"

She backed up until she was next to me. "Guidebook. Yes. Read."

It took her a few minutes to be able to drag her gaze from the city (which I thought was pretty cool at night—it really was pretty with all the lights on), but eventually she hauled out the guidebook and started reading about Notre Dame. Most of it was boring stuff, but she finally got to the gargoyles.

"That's not a gargoyle," she said as I wandered over to a big stone bird with an open beak that was clinging to the stone railing. There were metal barriers here, too, evidently to keep people from throwing themselves off the top. "The book says that only the gargoyles have a function—they drain the rainwater off the various roofs and buttresses. The rest are chimera, which are fantastical creatures that were added during a restoration in the nineteenth century. This is the chimeras' gallery, and it's . . . Oh! It's sixty-nine meters to the top, Emily! Three hundred and eighty-seven steps!"

"It didn't seem so bad to me," I said calmly, hoping she wasn't going to go all deranged on me. I walked down a narrow gallery with stone railings on either side to the south tower, and examined the chimeras. One of them was leaning its head on its hands as it stuck its tongue out at the city. I gave it a pat. "Come on; this one is harmless. You stand here and I'll take your picture."

Oh, rats, Olivier is here to hear me do my French drill. Be back as soon as he's gone.

Hugs and kisses,
~Em

Subject: Sorry!
From: EmInParis@parisstudy.com
To: Dru@seattlegrrl.com
Date: 13 April 2004 11:33 am

Back! And Olivier didn't try any of his octopus hands stuff on me, although he did try to look down my top. What a dirty old man!

OK, back to the saga of Emily and Holly. It's just getting good, too. Or rather, bad, depending on your point of view, and from where I was, it was bad, very bad, but you're not supposed to say that when you're telling someone something because then they know what to expect and it ruins the surprise. Foreshadowing, Mom says it's called, and she reads a lot of mysteries, so she's probably right.

Anyhoodles, there we were in Chimera Land. It took me five minutes to talk Holly into walking down the narrow gallery over to the south tower, but finally we did the picture thing with a couple of the chimeras. The gallery narrowed as it went around the tower, which was pretty slick, but I didn't stay long to look at the stone statues because Holly absolutely refused to see them. I took pictures, then came back to where she was standing, with her back against a wall, between two signs, one pointing left to the exit, the other pointing right, to another tower. "Oooh! I bet the gargoyles are up higher."

I slid a questioning glance at her. Holly looked like she wanted to ralph, but she mumbled something about making it to the top if it killed her, which it probably would.

"You're such a drama queen," I teased as we started up another staircase, this one even narrower than the last. It was wood, not stone, though, and wasn't nearly as long as the previous ones. In no time we popped out into a small room with a huge bell.

"Quasimodo's bell," Holly said in a whisper. "Oh, Em, don't!"

I couldn't help but reach around the big wooden beams housing the bell and rapping on it. It made a dull, low, heavy sort of sound, not at all bell-like. "Coolio! I've touched the Quasimodo bell!"

Holly angled the guidebook to catch the weak light of

the single bulb that lit the room. "This must be the belfry. The bell is named Emmanuel. I suppose you want to go on to the summit?"

"Yup," I said, and almost had to drag her up the last flight of stairs. It was really narrow, only room for one person at a time, but at last we made the top. Holly refused to look out at the view, and I have to admit that it was a bit cold up there at night, so I just looked around quickly, took a few pictures of the flying buttresses that were lit up from the ground, and started back down.

"See? That wasn't so bad," I said as we thumped down the wooden staircase. "And no one was the wiser. Now we can go back home and call the cops and get them working on your stolen passport and wallet."

Holly didn't say anything until we passed the bell and skirted the south tower to take the exit stairs. "I know you think it's good for me to try different things, Em, but I think I'll keep my different-thing-trying to places that aren't three hundred and eighty-seven steps up."

I laughed (it was a lot easier going down than up) and promised her I wouldn't do any more tower climbing. Everything was rosy until we came down to the first level, the one with the gift shop. A door I didn't remember seeing was closed. "Almost there," I said over my shoulder as I reached for the door.

It didn't open.

"I'm glad of that. I'm hungry, and I want the police to look for Mum's sweater."

I turned the knob of the door again, pulling on it a bit harder. It was probably just stuck.

"Em?"

I turned the knob the other way. "Beastly door, it's . . . uh . . . stuck."

Are you foreshadowing yet? 'Cause I bet you are; you're not stupid.

"Stuck? What do you mean, stuck?" Holly asked, her voice going higher with each word.

"Maybe stuck like it's locked," I said slowly, turning to face her. "I think someone came up and locked the door while we were in the other tower."

"Locked? LOCKED?" Holly shoved me aside and rattled the doorknob. "We can't be locked in; you told me we wouldn't be."

She pounded on the door, but it wouldn't budge. That's another thing those medieval builders were keen on—really solid doors. "It is locked! We're stuck here! We're locked in! No one knows we're here, Emily!"

The look on her face made me feel horrible. She was truly scared, and to be completely honest, Dru, at that moment I wasn't feeling terribly brave. What made me feel worse, though, is that I had promised her we wouldn't get into trouble, and here we were, locked in Notre Dame with no way out. "I'm sorry, Holly, I really am. I didn't know there was a door there. I didn't think—"

She turned on me and started yelling. "That's right, you didn't think! You never do, Emily; you just go off on wild hares and do stupid things, and then act surprised later when they turn into disasters! You just don't think, do you?" She slumped back against the door to the gift shop, pulling her knees up and wrapping her arms around her legs.

I stood there for a minute feeling like a great big idiot, then set Jack down next to her. I couldn't yell back at her because she was right. I don't like admitting it, but the whole thing with us being stuck there was my fault, just like having to drag Jack everywhere was my fault.

Boy, I really hate this being-adult-and-admitting-your-mistakes stuff.

"I'm going to go make sure there's not a back door anywhere. You'll be OK here by yourself?"

"I'm going to have to be, aren't I?" she said in a quavery voice, like she was going to cry.

I didn't say anything else, just started back up the stairs. I looked everywhere, but there was nothing, no hidden janitor's closet with a phone, no other stairway down, no key lying around just waiting to be used to unlock the door to the last flight of stairs, nothing. Just a lot of stone and chimeras. I stood on the chimera gallery and yelled for help, but it was so windy that I was sure no one heard me. Besides, who was there to hear? It was almost nine at night, and everyone had gone home. The only people left were probably snuggled up in the offices of the cathedral, not standing outside looking up at the gallery to see if any stupid American tourist had gotten herself and her girlfriend stuck up there.

Just in case anyone was looking, I peeled off my sweat-shirt (white) and stood shivering in my tee while I waved it around like a white flag. No police zoomed in or anything, so after I was turned to a block of ice I put it back on and went downstairs.

"I'm afraid we're stuck here," I said to the curled-up ball of misery that was Holly. She sat in the dim pool of light that glowed through the gift-shop windows. "I'm really sorry, Hol. You're right: I wasn't thinking. It was stupid to come up here when the tours were closed. I wish I could change it, but I can't. If it makes you feel better, though, I feel terrible about the whole thing, and I won't blame you at all if you don't want to see anything else in Paris with me."

"Oh, Em," Holly said, and lifted her face up from where it was resting on her knees. She was crying—no surprise there. (I felt a bit weepy myself.) "I'm sorry; I had no right to say what I did. I was just upset. Please forgive me."

I sat down beside her and hauled Jack over to my lap. "There's nothing to forgive. You're right, I do tend to act without thinking. Mom is always warning me about that, but I thought she was just legally obligated to say that, since she is my mother and all. I didn't think it was really true."

"It's not; I was wrong," Holly said, squeezing my hand. "You're right about me, though. I'm too timid sometimes, but I'm trying to get better."

"You're fine just the way you are; it's me who has to

change," I said, feeling like it was a Disney sort of moment. I half expected singing mice and birds to swoop down on us and sing a happy little song about undying, eternal friendship, but there was nothing around us but a whole lot of dark, so we just sat huddled together and talked about what our BFs were doing at that exact moment.

About an hour later the true horror of our situation hit.

"Em?"

"Huh?"

We were still propped up next to the gift shop. We'd run out of BF talk and were now going over everyone in school, and what we would wish on them if we were witches and could cast spells.

"I have to go to the loo."

"Oh. Um. I don't think there are any here. Can't you hold it? They're sure to unlock the door in the morning. What time did the guidebook say the tours start?"

Holly sighed. "Eight A.M."

"Poop. And it's only ten now?"

She pulled her sleeve up to look at her watch. "Ten after ten. That's ten hours we'll have to wait."

"Can you hold it that long?" I asked, feeling a bit pervy asking it, but hey, it was an emergency. I didn't think she'd mind me inquiring into her bladder strength under the circumstances.

"I'll try."

Two minutes later I had to go, too.

"The cow!" I said standing up. I peered in through the

glass of the gift shop window. "I bet they have a bathroom in there for employees."

"The door's locked, though; we tried it."

I gnawed on my lip for a minute or two, but no brilliant idea came to me. "I know you'll probably yell at me and tell me I'm being stupid again, but we could break into the gift shop and use the bathroom."

Holly looked horrified. "That would be illegal."

"Yeah, but if we didn't steal anything, and explained later that we really had to go, they probably wouldn't do anything to us except make us pay for breaking in."

Holly wrapped her arms around her legs again. "I'd rather just wait."

"OK," I said, sitting back down next to her.

Jack started crying then, so I was busy for a while feeding him the last little bit of water in his bottle, and changing his diapers. I didn't have any dry ones with me, just the pair I had changed earlier, which were still damp (usually I lay them out to dry before putting them back on him). That took about half an hour. By then I really, really, *really* had to pee.

"I'm going to break in. If I don't, I'll be sitting in a great big puddle."

"Oh, Em, don't! It's bad enough we're here, but breaking into a gift shop is a *crime!*"

I squirmed around. "I don't know if I can make it another ten hours."

"We're down to nine now. It won't be so bad. Maybe

if we talk about something exciting, it will get our minds off having to use the loo."

I squirmed around. "Exciting like what?"

"Well, you could tell me what you and Devon are going to do in Paris."

"Go on a canal boat for a romantic evening dinner, see the Virgin Megastore, see the underground bone place, have sex, go to the Moulin Rouge so we can pretend we're Nicole Kidman and Ewan McGregor, and if I don't get to the bathroom in the next ten seconds, my bladder is going to burst."

I got to my feet and tried the door to the gift shop. It was locked, natch.

"What are you going to do?" Holly asked in a breathy sort of whisper.

"I could kick down the door like they do in the movies," I said, pulling Jack from the baby backpack. I peeled off my sweatshirt and tee, then put the sweatshirt back on and wrapped the tee around Jack's neck like it was a neck brace. "But since it's usually guys or Xena or someone who does that, I think I'll go the easy route and break the glass next to the door so I can reach through and unlock it." I turned my head so I wouldn't get flying glass in my eyes, and swung Jack at the glass. His head was evidently hard enough, because there was a huge crash of glass. I looked back to see a big Jack's-head-sized hole in the glass next to the door. "Brother will scream about having to pay for the glass—and I'm sure he'll take it out of my allowance for the next fifty years—but it's better

115

than hiring someone to mop up the puddle of piddle on the floor."

"I suppose so, although I still think it's wrong. But I really do have to use the loo," Holly said as she got to her feet.

I checked Jack over, but he didn't look like he had suffered anything that would register as abuse, although he had a long gash on the top of his head, and one eye had popped out. I pocketed the eye, figuring I'd glue it back in later. The gash was a bit more diffy, but right then was not the moment to worry over what I'd tell Horseface. I unwound the tee and used it to push off the shards of glass so I could reach through and unlock the door.

A minute later I had the door open.

Two minutes later we discovered that the gift shop *didn't* have a bathroom.

Five minutes after that I found a cleaning bucket under the cash register. I held it up to show her. "Behold, the emergency Notre Dame loo," I said.

Holly was back to looking horrified. "I couldn't!"

I looked at it and grimaced. I knew how she felt. "There's nothing else, Holly. It's that or find a dark corner, or hold it, and I'm doing the pee-pee dance, here. I have to *go*."

"You go, then," she said, turning her back. "I won't watch."

I looked at the bucket. I set it down. I found a couple of paper towels and set them next to the bucket. "OK. I'm going to go. It's just a bucket, after all."

116

Holly hurried out of the gift shop to stand outside the door. I got out of my jeans and stood there looking at the bucket. I stood over it. I grabbed the paper towels, telling myself there was no other choice.

"Damn!" I grabbed my jeans and pulled them on again, and stormed out of the room. "You go."

"Did you—" she said, not meeting my eye.

"No. I couldn't. But that doesn't mean you can't."

"You go first. It will be less . . . ooky . . . for you that way."

Ick. I didn't even want to think about that. "I can't. I tried. I think my mom toilet-trained me too hard or something, because I can't pee in a bucket."

Holly sighed. "Oh, I'm glad to hear you say that, because I can't, Emily, I just can't. Not in a bucket."

A half an hour of pacing back and forth (we couldn't sit without dancing) and we changed our minds. I won't go into the details, but trust me when I say that I'm never, ever entering a church again without peeing first.

In other words, it was ew[3].

We spent the rest of the night trying to sleep, but we didn't. For one, it was too cold. They don't heat those towers! And for another, it was too hard on the floor to sleep. Jack wanted to be fed in the morning, but his bottle was empty, so I poured some of the window cleaning fluid from the bottle I found in the (unused, at that point) bucket in the gift shop. The cleaner was blue, and I figured it wouldn't hurt Jack, but it stained his lips and

117

mouth blue, not to mention his little thingy and butt when it came out the other end.

By six we were running up and down the stairs trying to get warm. When eight came and a man and a woman unlocked the door, we were sitting outside the broken window with our explanations rehearsed until they were perfect.

Almost.

Gotta run. I'm supposed to show Olivier my translation before lunch and do a fake conversation between two girls who want to buy the same purse and I don't have much time. Will tell you the rest later.

Kissies and hugsies,
~Em

Subject: Re: Oh. My. God.
From: EmInParis@parisstudy.com
To: Dru@seattlegrrl.com
Date: 14 April 2004 7:22 am

Dru wrote:
> *I don't know where to start, there's just so much! OK,*
> *I do know—EW EW EW! You peed in a* bucket?

Let's just pretend that never happened, OK?

> *happened when they found you and Holly? And did*
> *you get into trouble about the broken window? But*

> *most important of all, WHAT DID YOU DO WITH THE*
> *BUCKET???*

You're obsessing about that bucket, aren't you? We didn't get into *trouble* trouble about the window, although the head priest guy yelled at us in Latin for a bit until the police got there and Holly explained everything in French. Then Madame came to get us, and she yelled at us for a while in English. I liked it better when I couldn't understand the yelling. I called Brother when we got back and told him he had to cough up some money for our incarceration in Notre Dame. Surprisingly, he took it pretty well. He just said, "I'm surprised that's all it will cost me. I assumed that with you loose in Paris, I'd owe close to the national debt by now."

Fathers!

> *You* peed *in a bucket?*

Moving on (unlike *some* people) . . .

> *Holly get her stuff back? What did the police say about*
> *the* gamins? *Honestly, Em, only you could go to Paris*
> *and get* gamin*ed and* clochard*ed.*

I'd like to point out that Holly was with me; thus it wasn't just me these horrible things happened to. No, no sign of the money and passport and her mom's sweater, but the police took down a description of everything that

119

happened, and evidently told Holly they would watch that area and see if the *gamins* returned. Madame took her to the Thomas Cook office to get her traveler's checks replaced, so at least she has money again.

> *Nothing is going on here. Rachel fell off a horse and*
> *broke her arm. My mother is still certifiable and will*
> *not let me go to NYC with Kimo and Sam. Timothy*
> *and I went on a date Sunday, and he got his hand*
> *under my shirt and touched my nipple, but that's all.*
> *Oh, this is very cool—I swam the two-hundred-meter*
> *freestyle in 2.07.90! It's not a pool record, but close.*

The cow, girl! You had a nipple touch and swam almost a pool record and you call that nothing? Tell all about the date with Tim. And sign my name on Rach's cast for me.

   Gotta run. I have *beaucoup* (that means a lot) of *travail* (work) to do before *petit déjeuner* (breakfast) because we lost a day, what with all the being yelled at and police and stuff. Oh, before I go, I have to give you your helpful French phrase for the day, courtesy of Pascal. I told him about Devon coming on Saturday, and asked for something to call him, because Devon (like everyone else in England) speaks French. He looked thoughtful for a moment, then said, "What do you want to call him?"

   "What do you mean? Oh, like 'sweetheart'? Um . . . what's something girls call cute guys here?"

   He grinned. "*Poulet.*"

"Chicken?" I asked (and go, me, for my fabulous knowledge of French that I didn't need it translated). "Girls call guys chicken? Isn't that an insult?"

"No, no, it is sweet, very affectionate. Romantic."

"Oh, well that's what I want. So I just call him *poulet*?"

He shook his head. "No, you would say *ma petite poupoulet en sucre*. That is 'my little sugar chicky-wicky.' "

My little sugar chicky-wicky! Isn't French just the coolest language ever? "Coolio! Thanks, Pascal."

"If you want to really be romantic, you can say *ma petite poupoulet en susucre*. That would be my little sugary-wugary chicky-wicky."

I hooted; I just had to. Isn't that just the funniest? "That's it, that's exactly what I want to call him. Sugary-wugary chicky-wicky. Absotively perfect!"

Pascal tipped his head on the side. "Absotively?"

"Yeah. It's like absolutely, positively—absotively, get it?"

"Got it," he said, and toddled off to help with the intermediate class.

Oops! Been too long. Have to go write out my stupid dialogue again. Olivier is coming to check it before breffy. Later, alligator!

Hs and Ks,
~Em

P.S. Your Very Cool French of the day is *ma petite poupoulet en susucre*. Use it in at least three sentences. Quiz on Friday!

Subject: Re: Hey, Fang!
From: EmInParis@parisstudy.com
To: Fbaxter@oxfordshire.agricoll.co.uk
Date: 15 April 2004 9:17 pm

Fbaxter wrote:
> *only girl I know who can get herself locked into a major*
> *cathedral. But as usual, you came through with flying*
> *colors. No surprise there, eh?*

Yeah, well, Holly was right about me not thinking before I act. I realize that now, although you know, I thought that being an adult and all, it wouldn't hurt having someone say you were wrong—and admitting it—but it does. It sucks. I *hate* being wrong!

How's the new job going? Is the vet you're working under nice? What sorts of vet-in-training-wheels sorts of things are you doing? You haven't had to kill anyone's beloved dog yet, have you? I think being a vet would be good except for that. And the surgery (ick, ick, ick!). And seeing animals who are abused. And run over. And other bad stuff like that.

Tonight is disco night here at Chez Strange (you have to say that with a French accent so the word *strange* comes out like "strahnge"). We're supposed to dress up in seventies hippie stuff and dance to real disco songs, but I'm thinking that it's, like, against my religion or something, because I just can't do it. It's just all so John Travolta, you know? So old!

Anyhoodles, I hope you're doing well and everything is going good and all. I miss you something terrible! It's just no fun having to only do e-mail and not be able to call you up and talk.

Big smoochy kisses,

Emily

Subject: Yay with whipped cream on top!
From: EmInParis@parisstudy.com
To: DevTheMan@britnet.co.uk
Date: 16 April 2004 7:22 am

I'm going to see you tomorrow! Yay!

Hugs, hugs, HUGS!!!
Emily

Subject: Re: What about Pascal?
From: EmInParis@parisstudy.com
To: Dru@seattlegrrl.com
Date: 17 April 2004 12:01 pm

Dru wrote:
> *about Pascal? Won't you feel all, like, weird around*
> *him with Devon? I mean, he has been giving you*
> *survival French and stuff on the side, and I really think*
> *he likes you, not that you think so (you're so blind*
> *about these things, Em). Are you going to avoid him*
> *when you've got Devon with you?*

OK, first of all, Pascal does not like me. Well, he does, but not in a GF sort of way. I'd know that, despite you thinking I'm blind (I'm *so* not blind!). So there's nothing to do about Pascal. Devon said he'd come with me to the seventies dance tonight—did I tell you that other French schools are coming as well, so there'll be more people than just our gang—but besides that, I don't think Devon and Pascal will meet much. Holly is going to pal around with the GTs while I'm Devoning, which I'm going to be doing every waking moment when I'm not stuck in the library reading Paris *Vogue* and watching the stupid language tapes. (I think one of the women on the language tape soap opera is pregnant with her sister's husband's baby, but I'm not sure. It's either that, or her washing machine is broken. French is such a weird language!)

Anyhoodles, Devon should be getting into Paris soon. Holly and I are going to the train station to meet him (have to take Holly because I flunked the survival French pop quiz Olivier sprang on me yesterday), which is kind of a bummer. It's not that I don't want Holly there, but with her standing around being all BF-less, and missing Ruaraidh—not that she gets to see him all that much even when she is home, but she says being in a different country makes it a whole lot worse, which is just silly when you think about it, because Scotland *is* a different country than England—where was I, got lost? . . . Oh, yeah, Devon. Anyhoo, with Holly standing around, I can't throw myself in his manly arms and kiss his face and tell him he's my sugary-wugary chicky-wicky and all that stuff. But that's OK; I'll be able to tell him that tonight.

> *I'm thinking that I should change my name to Connor.*
> *Connor is a nice name, don't you think? Connor*
> *Chance. CC. I'd be CC.*

Um. How do I say this . . . Connor is a guy's name! Do you really want to have people thinking you're a guy? I was thinking about thinking about Helen, but that sounds so old-fashioned; then I saw it written in French, and it's Helene. Isn't that pretty? Helene Marie Williams. Hmm. Must think on it.

> *How was disco night?*

We didn't go. I know, I know, there I was making a big stink about disco and all, but I heard S-Bee telling one of the German girls that the really cool spot to hang out at night is the steps in front of Sacré Coeur (it's another cathedral).

"What do you think about us going there tonight?" I asked Holly as we were out shopping for seventies disco stuff. I wasn't having any luck, although Holly found a cute peasant skirt and ruffly top. "S-Bee told Trudy that there are street entertainers and stuff. And later people go down the street to a cabaret called the Chien Agile. It's supposed to be historic and all. That sounds like a lot more fun than standing around watching a bunch of

American and English kids dance, don't you think?"

"A cabaret?" Holly asked, her eyes doing the startled deer-in-headlights thing (no one does scared as well as she does). "I thought Devon was taking us to the Moulin Rouge on Wednesday?"

"Yeah, but that's a different sort of cabaret. Bee said that at the Chien Agile, the audience gets to be part of the show. You get to sing songs and stuff. That sounds like it would be fun, huh? A whole lot more fun than some majorly lame dance."

"Well . . ." Holly said, and I knew then that I had her. When she starts off a sentence with "well," it means she's caving.

"Good! I'll go tell Madame that we're going to Sacré Coeur instead of the disco."

"Y'all going to another church? After what happened to y'all at Notre Dame?" a Southern voice twanged behind me. "Why?"

Now, I know what you're thinking. You're wondering why I haven't said anything about the GTs setting us up to be locked into Notre Dame. The truth is, I'm not sure whether they did or not. Holly says no, they didn't, it was just a coincidence that they were standing around waiting to distract the priest while we slipped upstairs to see the gargoyles, but I say that the proof is in the pudding. (OHMIGOD! Now I'm spouting Mom-isms! Eek! I'm turning ANCIENT!!!) Anyway, the proof is in the fact that neither GT said anything to Madame when we didn't show up for bed check that night. I asked them later why

126

they didn't tell the police (who Madame called right away) where we were, and Sephora said it was so we wouldn't get into trouble.

Yeah, right. Like I'm going to believe that? Any-hoodles, there was Sabine drawling at my back while I was convincing Holly that we needed to go stair-sitting and cabaret-ing that night.

"Emily says it's cool to sit on the steps and watch the lights come on all over Paris," Holly said. I pinched her so she wouldn't say anything more, but it was too late. "Then afterward everyone goes to a cabaret and sings."

"Oooh," Sephora said, coming over to where Holly and I were flaked out on the white wrought-iron chairs in the courtyard. The chairs aren't very comfy—they leave marks on your legs if you wear shorts or a skirt—but it's a fabu spot with a couple of trees and spiral stairs up to the bedroom, and little tables and stuff. Very trendy. "Thayat sounds like so much fun! What do you think, Beanie? Should we go with them or go to the disco?"

"Where is this Sacruh Core?" Beanie (hoot!) asked.

"Montmarte," Holly answered. She knows all that stuff, having read the guidebook to Paris that the school sent us.

"Isn't that where a whole bunch of people were hanged?" Sephora asked in a really interested tone.

I groaned. If there was anything even remotely creepy about a spot, the GTs wanted to see it.

"I don't know—" Holly started to say.

"We'll come with y'all," the twins said together.

So that's how we ended up going with them to sit on the steps of the Sacré Coeur. I will give S-Bee this—she was right about it being very cool. The church is on top of a big hill, and it has a great view of the city. And there were lots of excellent street entertainers there—a band from Peru that played those pipe thingies old people like to listen to (luckily they were finishing up just as we arrived), a couple of guys with acoustic guitars who did Beatles songs, and a couple of contortionists. The only bad performers were the mimes—they were everywhere! You couldn't take a step without bumping into one of them doing their stupid mime stuff. Evidently the hip thing in the mime world is to pretend to be a statue. They only move a tiny little bit when someone drops money into the box or whatever at their feet. A couple of them were dressed up to look like white statues; one was the Statue of Liberty (did you know it was made in France? I didn't!); and there was even a pair that was dressed up like they were getting married. It was awful, but Holly and I did have a fun half hour mocking them in whispers, so the GTs wouldn't hear us. They thought the mimes were fabu. *As if!*

Oh! I took this picture of this really cool old man who was playing one of those hurdy-gurdy thingies. On the ground next to him was the cutest little doll bed with blankies and pillows, and a green stuffed bunny, and lying on it back-to-back was a fat dachshund and a gray-and-white-striped cat. Holly almost cried when I dragged her away from them, but you know how she is about animals. We both put a bunch of euros in the guy's hat which made Holly feel better.

We bought a bag of bread crumbs to feed the sparrows (Holly got them to land on her hand and eat right off of her fingers, but I got all weird when they fluttered around me and just put the crumbs on the ground for them), and watched people and stuff until it got dark and the lights came on. It was nice and all, but I wasn't totally blown away like everyone swore I would be.

"There it is," Sabine said a little while later when we were walking to the Chien Agile. "Oh, isn't it cute? But where do you suppose the gallows stood thayat hung all those bad people?"

Holly and I rolled our eyes, and took pictures of each other standing in front of the famous Chien Agile building. It was an old stone house separated from the rest of the buildings, painted bright Pepto-Bismol pink, with emerald green shutters and doors. The sign hanging outside showed a dog leaping over a rabbit jumping out of a pan, which Holly said was painted by some famous guy, and is what gave the cabaret the name. We had to wait about twenty minutes to get in because there was a line, but even so, we got a table near the front, which was very cool.

We ordered our drinks (Holly had a Lemon Squash, I had a Coke, and the GTs made a big fuss about getting bottled water so they wouldn't get the trots); then Holly read to us about the history of the cabaret. Seems a whole lot of famous writers and stuff used to hang out there.

"That's all really nice and all, but the important question is what y'all are going to sing." Sabine interrupted Holly. "Sephie and I love to karaoke. We do a killer version of 'My Heart Will Go On.' It makes Daddy cry evruh time."

I put my hand over my mouth and made noises like I was coughing, except I was really doing the "gag me because I'm going to fall over dead at any moment" move. Holly saw it and had to pretend she was blowing her nose so the GTs wouldn't see her laughing.

"I want to do 'Wannabe,' " Sephora said with a pout. "I just love those Spice Girls, don't y'all?"

"Uh, I'll take no for five hundred," I said, majorly cool and all because honestly—the Spice Girls? The Titanic song? I'd die rather than sing those!

"Oh, Sephie! Not 'Wannabe' again! She sang that all last year. Our daddy bought us a karaoke machine of our own," Sabine said like that was something good. Everyone knows those home karaoke machines are *so* Lame List!

"I don't want to sing," Holly said in a whisper while the GTs argued about which gacky song they wanted to do.

"You have a really good voice; you have to sing," I said, snagging the karaoke song book from Sabine when she leaned over to hiss in her sister's ear.

"I don't! I'll die if I have to sing alone!"

"Then we'll do it together, although I want brownie points for doing it with you, because your voice is much nicer than mine. Mine breaks up a lot and yours always sounds like it's singing the right notes."

"You have a lovely voice," Holly said, all fierce and stuff, which was really very sweet because, as you know, I don't. Brother once told me that when I sing I sound like bullfrogs being spitted on hot skewers, but you know how fathers are.

I let Holly hold Jack while I looked through the book of songs. We picked out two to sing—"Love Shack" and "I'm Too Sexy." After a while, one of the owners of the cabaret came up and explained in French, English, and German what was going to happen. They should have had Japanese too, because almost the whole club was filled with Japanese tourists. Anyhoodles, there were a few acts—two singers, one dancing couple, and a French comedian who Holly said wasn't very funny—then they opened up the stage to the audience.

Remember that karaoke thing that Rachel had at her birthday party two years ago? We had fun at that, right? Well, the Chien Agile didn't do quite the same sort of karaoke. They wanted the people singing to entertain the audience, so that meant you gave the waitress your list of songs, and they called you backstage while the song before you was being sung. They had a huge area with all sorts of trunks of costumes, and dressed everyone up for their songs, whipping around cardboard scenery and stuff to go with the outfits. The GTs were up right away

131

with their *Titanic* song. They both wore long old-time dresses and big poofy wigs that were made of stuff that didn't even remotely look like real hair, and stood in front of a painted ship backdrop.

"This is too funny," I told Holly as the audience roared with laughter. The stage guys had these blue cardboard waves that rocked back and forth in front of the GTs as they sang. The funny part was that the waves kept getting higher and higher, like S&S were sinking, until finally all you could see were waves, and Sabine and Sephora making little hopping jumps to see over the waves while they sang the finish. "Now, *that* is what I call good stuff!"

Holly looked horrified as she glanced around us. Everyone in the audience was still laughing over the GTs' drowning, even after the stage guys had herded them off the stage so they could set up for the next song. "What do you think they'll do to *us?*"

"Nothing mean, Hol. It's just a bit of fun. I promise you'll have a good time. You love to sing!"

She didn't say anything, but she had her worried look on, and not even holding Jack in his cute blue Nehru jacket made her happy. A couple of minutes later, Sabine and Sephora came stomping back to our table, arguing viciously.

"You were too off-key!" Sabine snapped as she sat down at our table.

"Well, if I was, it was this stupid club's fault. Imagine blocking us with those stupid waves! They obviously don't know how to do karaoke at all, but what can I expect? We're in *Paris.*" Sephora plopped down in her chair and glared around at everyone.

"Stupid French people," Sabine agreed. "They don't do anything right he-yuh. Back home everyone knows how to do karaoke properly."

"Yeah, but this isn't Bumsquat, Georgia," I said, really embarrassed because some of the Japanese tourists sitting next to us heard them. This is exactly the sort of stuff Brother means when he talks about being a good American. "And you heard Holly when she read out the bit from the menu about people who volunteer entertaining the audience. That's what happened—you entertained."

"They made fun of us," Sephora snarled, sending me a glare that probably could have dropped a horse. "That's not entertaining."

"I dunno, I thought it was pretty funny when you guys were hopping around trying to see over the waves."

"I'm sure as shootin' goin' to tell Daddy about this," Sabine said, ignoring me.

"Just you wait until it's *your* turn," Sephora added with a really evil grin. Right at that moment the waitress came up and said something to Holly.

"It's time for us to go," she whispered.

Sephora's grin got a whole lot eviler.

"If you keep that up, your face will freeze that way," I said as I got up to follow Holly. The GT said something that I won't repeat because it's anatomically impossible, and besides, I'm not a potty mouth.

We went backstage and were instantly smothered by

a couple of the costume people, who threw two gingham checked country dresses over our heads. Holly got an orangy wig with ponytails, while I got a black wig with two long braids. The dresses were cut down the back and had Velcro tabs, so you could wear them over your own clothes, although I had to roll my jeans up to my knees so they wouldn't show.

One of the women said something to Holly, then turned to me and said in a really heavy accent, "The doll, it must stay here."

I had set Jack in his backpack down while I was getting dressed. "Sorry, no can do. If he starts crying while we're out there, it'll show up as neglect."

"Neglect?" the woman asked, frowning down at Jack.

"It's a long story. You'll just have to believe me when I say I have to keep him with me."

The woman pursed her lips for a minute, then laughed and said something to a friend. They got a pillowcase and put Jack (minus backpack) into it, and stuffed it under my gingham dress like I was pregnant.

As soon as the song before us ("Come Dancing," which had a bunch of girls doing cancans behind the guy singing it) was done, they pushed out a shack backdrop, and Holly and I went out to sing "Love Shack." Other than me being pregnant with Jack, I had no idea what they were going to do to us while we sang. People giggled when they saw me, but it wasn't uproariously funny like the bit with the GTs was. Holly kept looking around us, barely singing until I pinched her arm, and then she got into it. Just as we started on the chorus, the door to the backdrop popped open and a girl with a pregnant tummy jumped out.

By the time we got through the whole song, there were eight girls, all with pillows stuffed under their dresses. Love Shack, get it? Hahahahah. Anyway, right at the end, when I sang, "Tin roof, rusted," one of the girls offstage made giving-birth gestures, so I lay down on the floor, and screamed in time to the "bang, bang!" parts as I reached under my dress and pulled Jack out.

Everyone was hysterical by that point, because the pillow girls started pulling out little baby dolls, too. Just as the song ended, Jack started crying, so I ran to my backpack and dashed back out with his bottle. People loved it. We took three curtain calls. THREE!

"Thayat was just disgustin'," Sephora said when we got back to the table. She had a look on her face like she was smelling cabbage cooking. Or maybe dog poop. Whatever, it was a nasty face. "Pulling your baby doll out like that—it was just pure-D dis-gus-ting!"

"It sure enough was," Sabine, said, nodding. "Ah'm just surprised you went along with that, Holly. You don't seem like the disgusting type to me."

"It wasn't disgusting; it was a parody," Holly said at the same time I said, "Disgusting, my butt!"

Poop, gotta run. We were supposed to leave ten

minutes ago to get Devon. Tell me all about what you and the rest of the guys are doing this weekend!

Hugs and kissies,
~Em

Subject: Thanks mucho!
From: EmInParis@parisstudy.com
To: Hwilliams@mediev-l.oxford.co.uk
Date: 18 April 2004 12:47 am

I got the birthday card today—thanks for the money, Brother! You and Mom might be ancient, but you're still cool. Most of the time.

Yes, Devon got here today. Holly and I went to the train station to pick him up. He's taking me to dinner tomorrow night at a really expensive restaurant, which is really fabu, don't you think? And stop wrinkling your unibrow like I know you are—I'm not going to get drunk again, OK? Sheesh! You make one little mistake and get stinking drunk, and you're never allowed to forget it. I mean, really, isn't it, like, your job to forgive and forget? Maybe you need to bone up on the Parental Unit Handbook or something, because it's, like, *way* over the line to put, *Don't get drunk again like you did the last time you went to a party with Devon*, in someone's birthday card.

Um. Thanks for the money, though. I need it. Jack's baby stuff has cost more than I thought. See you in a week!

Emily

Subject: You are condom obsessed!
From: EmInParis@parisstudy.com
To: BessWill@btinternet.co.uk
Date: 18 April 2004 12:52 am

Hey, Bess, thanks for the card and the Virgin gift certificate. We're going to the Megastore in a couple of days, so I'll be able to use it then.

And as for the condoms . . . um, excuse me, do I look like a ho? Cause you gave me enough for a whole army of prostitutes! And who told you I was going to need them? I know it wasn't Holly, because she's not like that. OHMIGOD, it wasn't your witch friend, was it? Did she read my mind and know that Devon and I are going to do it for my birthday? EEEK! What else did she say? And will you please tell her for me that I think it's totally wrong for her to go around reading people's personal thoughts about having sex without asking?

Later, chick.

Emily

Subject: Re: Dru has sent you a Wicked Posty o' Fun
From: EmInParis@parisstudy.com
To: Dru@seattlegrrl.com
Date: 18 April 2004 9:34 am

That was TOO FUNNY! Thank you for the hottie birthday card; I loved it. I'm forwarding it to Bess so she can print it out on the color ink-jet.

I'm seventeen! Yay! I'm going to do it! Yaaaaa-aaaaaaaaaay! Will tell you more later, after the deed is done.

I feel so worldly. I think I may write a poem or something.

Seventeen-year-old hugsies,
~Em

Subject: Aw, Fang!
From: EmInParis@parisstudy.com
To: Fbaxter@oxfordshire.agricoll.co.uk
Date: 18 April 2004 9:36 am

Thank you a gazillion times for the pretty cloisonné flower necklace. It's gorgeous! I love it! You're just the sweetest thing on two legs. I'll wear it tonight, when Devon takes me out to dinner for my birthday. I wish you could be here, too—I miss you terribly. Don't forget to e-mail me and tell me what's going on. I miss my Fang chats!

Hugs and oodles of kisses,
Emily

Subject: Re: WHAT HAPPENED???
From: EmInParis@parisstudy.com
To: Dru@seattlegrrl.com
Date: 19 April 2004 12:40 pm

Dru wrote:

> *You have to tell me everything, EVERYTHING—what*
> *you did, and what he did, and what it felt like, and all*
> *that stuff that no one really tells you. You're my*
> *absolute best friend in the whole wide world, so you*
> *HAVE to tell me. It's a law. So tell. Right now. I'm*
> *waiting. WHERE ARE YOU???*

sigh

I'm here. Yesterday was one of the longest days of my life, and that includes the day in third grade when I got my head stuck between the gym wall and the drainpipe, and the fire department had to come and saw the pipe off to get me out.

OK, I'm not going to do any of that foreshadowing stuff that Mom says ruins mysteries. I'm just going to tell it like it happened.

Oh, poop, that bit above is foreshadowing, isn't it? Well, ignore it. Pretend I never said it. Yesterday started out really good. Mom and Brother and Bess sent me birthday cards with money and a Virgin gift certificate, which I got on Saturday because there's no mail on Sunday, of course. Oh, and Fang sent me this absolutely gorgeous cloisonné flower necklace—I'll get a piccy of it when I go home. It's really pretty, and he sent a nice card with a kitten holding a cupcake, which was so sweet. I really miss him. Sometimes I think if I didn't have Devon . . . No, won't go there. It's not polite to think about another guy when you have a perfectly good BF who takes you out to dinner on your birthday and stuff.

We don't have to do French lessons on Sundays, so after breffy I told Madame that I was leaving for the day. I didn't tell her I wasn't going to be back that night, because that's, like, *so* against the rules unless you have your parents' permission, but I had heard a couple of days ago that Madame and Pascal were popping out to see her sick sister in Lyon (that's a town somewhere in France—don't know quite where) and they wouldn't be back until Monday. I had arranged it with Holly so she would do the pillows-in-bed thing to make it look like I was there in case Delphine checked. Clever, huh?

Yeah, well, that's what I thought, too.

Crap. I'm foreshadowing again. Forget that bit, as well, 'K?

"You are going by yourself?" Madame asked, all frowny and unhappy as she looked at me and Holly. "I was not aware that you passed the survival French test yet."

I shrugged. "I haven't, but my boyfriend, Devon, speaks French really well. He has an uncle who lives in Marseilles, and he comes over here a lot. We're going to go on a canal tour today, then out to dinner for my birthday." And later we were going to get busy with each other, but hey, if you think I told her *that* you're nuttier than a nutball on a pile of nut-crushed almonds! Hahahahahah!

"Hmm. Your parents, I take it that they know of your plans? They have met this boyfriend named Devon?"

"Oh, yeah, lots of times. He's been over to dinner four times. My mom likes him a lot."

"Hmm," she said again, but evidently my "Little Miss Innocent with no plans to have sex with Devon" face worked, because she just warned me to be back before curfew, and went off to line up the daily outings.

"Come to my room before you go," Holly said in a whisper, giving me a surprisingly wicked grin. "I have a birthday present for you."

"You didn't have to," I said, knowing that Holly's mom had to send her replacement money because the Cook's people wouldn't refund all of her lost traveler's checks. (She left most of the stubs in her purse with the traveler's checks, so she had no proof she had them.)

"I know, but I wanted to. It's an exciting day!"

"It will be later," I whispered back, and we gave in and had a few whispery giggles until Madame glared a "shut up" glare at us.

At the end of breakfast, everyone stood up and sang "Happy Birthday" to me, which was so embarrassing. I mean, what are you supposed to do while people are singing to you? I never know whether I should just stand there and smile gently, like I'm really touched they're singing, or to join in and sing, too, which is just silly, because who sings "Happy Birthday" to themselves? Anyhoo, once the HB ordeal was over and Madame gave me a French birthday card signed by everyone, I followed Holly upstairs to the room she shared with the GTs.

"Here. It's something for tonight," she said, handing me a wrapped box.

I shook it. It didn't sound like anything. "It's not condoms, is it? 'Cause Bess sent me a whole ton of them with the Virgin gift card—"

Holly's eyes got really big. "No, it isn't condoms. Open it."

I tried to be nice and admire the wrapping paper, but I was too curious to go on and on about it, like Mom says is polite. Inside it was a box with a bunch of bright pink tissue paper. I pulled out the tissue and discovered it wasn't paper—it was a silky nightie, one of those sexy ones called negligees. This one had cream-colored lace at the top, and was made of almost see-through gauzy pink material. There was a lace-and-pink robe thingy that went over it. It was absolutely FABULOUS!

"OHMIGOD, it's so great! It's much nicer than my red marabou baby doll, which is what I was going to wear, but this is so *über*ly wonderful! It looks much more adult! Thank you, Holly! Devon's going to wig out completely when he sees me in it!"

"It's really naughty," Holly said, all blushy and stuff. She gets so embarassed about sex, there's just *no* talking to her about it. "But I thought you might like it. The lady in the shop said the color is Barbie pink."

"Sometimes naughty is good, and Barbie pink is fantastic! I just love it. Thank you, thank you, thank you!" I did a little dance around Holly, holding up the negligee to my front. Unfortunately, I forgot just how snoopy the

GTs are, because suddenly there they were, standing in the door watching me do a Barbie-pink twirl.

"What's going on heeyuh?" Sabine asked. "What's that you have?"

"Oh!" Sephora gasped as she pushed into the room behind her twin. "It's one of those racy nighties! What are you going to do with it, Emily?"

"Tie it around my head and dance naked in the Place Concorde." I thought their eyes were going to bug out when I said that, hee! "It's a nightie, so duh, I'm going to wear it at night. When I'm in bed." With Devon. Ahem. No, I didn't say that out loud, although I wanted to flaunt Devon to them, but I couldn't, because flaunting him to them would also be flaunting him to Holly, and I already felt bad enough about leaving her while Dev and I went off and did the romantic thing together.

"Oh," Sephora said, but her eyes were all bright, like she didn't believe me. "It looks like it would be cold."

I didn't say anything to that, just thanked Holly again before I hurried back to my room and emptied out my big purse, stuffing it full of the nightie, undies, my red velvet coffin-lining dress (got it last month; it's the fabuest thing you've ever seen!), the birthday necklace Fang gave me, fishnets, and my ankle-strap platform heels. There wasn't much room left, so I had to shove Bess's condoms into Jack's backpack, along with his bottle and diapers.

By ten I was ready to go. By eleven I was majorly pissed.

"Maybe Devon got lost," Holly said as I paced back

and forth in the library. She had found me in there waiting for Devon, getting angrier and angrier as the whole day slipped by with us not being together.

"Devon? Mr. 'I've Been to Paris a Gazillion Times'? I don't think so. He probably slept in late or stopped to buy me a birthday something, or got distracted, or kidnapped by terrorists, or sucked into a portal to another dimension, or eaten by cats or something. How do I know? I'm just the girlfriend!"

"I'm sure it's something he couldn't help," Holly said in a scared whisper as I stomped up and down the library. "He's not normally late for dates."

"Only about half the time," I stormed. "The cow! It's after eleven! Oh, great, the boat tour leaves in three minutes! Now what are we going to do? Devon said this canal trip is really popular and he had to pay all sorts of money for the tickets so we could have lunch going down the Seine, and now it's all gone to hell in a handbasket! Well, all I can say is, he'd better be prepared to do some majorly huge groveling when he finally does show up, because my whole, entire birthday is hanging by a thread, and if he doesn't have proof of a broken arm, or tire marks from where he was run over, or a note from the police saying he was late because he was single-handedly saving a bus full of tourists from a deranged ax murderer, he's going to be meat. Dead meat. With worms on it!"

"Why worms? I would have thought maggots would be more appropriate," a guy's voice drawled from the doorway. I spun around and glared at Devon as he leaned against the door frame. He smiled, and you know how his smiles normally melt my insides? Well, something must have happened to me, because his smile was just as nice, but it didn't melt anything. "How about if I was held up by a train in the Metro that broke down? Would that do as an explanation, or do you want serious, on-the-knees groveling?"

Behind me, Holly giggled. That's when I went insane. No, seriously, I'm not kidding you, I think I had a insane attack or something, because I stood there looking at him, thinking that he was the most droolworthy guy I had ever seen, the sweetest, the nicest, and he'd done every-thing he promised he would do when we were in Scot-land and I gave him the terms of us being GF and BF together, and yet all of a sudden I realized that he wasn't *it*.

Have you ever heard of anything so stupid in your whole life? Not *it*? Devon? The hottest hottie around? He was *full* of "it"! He positively *oozed* "it"! He . . . was . . . it!

Except my insane brain kept whispering, "He's not, you know."

I hate it when my brain goes off and does stuff on its own, don't you? Anyhoodles, I told my brain to take the day off and let me handle things. "I would make you grovel, Devon, but we don't have time. Maybe the canal thingy is late. Maybe we can still make it if we take a taxi."

He was shaking his head even before I finished talking. "I've already called and switched our reservations to tonight. Instead of having lunch on the river and dinner out, we'll reverse the two. Here. These are for you. Happy birthday, love."

See, I told the insane part of my mind (must have got that part from Brother) as I took the bouquet of pretty purple and pink flowers he held out for me. *See? If he wasn't* it, *he wouldn't bring you flowers.*

My brain just rolled its eyes and pursed its lips while I went all girly over Devon's bringing me flowers. It took me a few minutes to find a vase to put them in, but right after I stuck them in my room I gathered up Jack and my stuffed-to-the-rim purse, and we toddled off to do the birthday thing.

No, not *that* thing! You need to wash your brain out with soap, chick. You've got a smutty, smutty mind. Devon took me to lunch at an outdoor café, where he asked me what I wanted to do. "I heard from a mate back home that everyone is into Rollerblading here. They close off some streets every Sunday afternoon and let people Rollerblade on them. How about we do that for a couple of hours, then go on the canal tour?"

We were sitting at a little black metal table on the Champs-Élysées, which is this very chichi street in Paris where all the big fashion places are. It's really pricey just to sit and have coffee (like $20 each!!!), but Devon said that anyone who was anyone had coffee there, so we did, too, which is just *über*fabu, don't you think?

"Um. Rollerblading. Um," I said, trying to make my insane mind sane again so it could figure out a way to

146

tell Devon that I've never Rollerbladed. If I told him, he'd want to know why, because everyone Rollerblades, but I'd die of mortification if I had to tell him about the incident during your ice-skating party. Damn my puny-ankle-muscle genes! I'm sure I get that from Brother, too.

"Good. Finish up and we'll go rent a pair of 'blades."

"Um," I said, but it was no use. I couldn't tell him my shameful secret. What sort of guy wants a girlfriend who can't ice-skate or Rollerblade? Devon was obviously looking forward to Rollerblading around Paris, and I didn't want to disappoint him. Not to mention having to explain the whole ankle thing to him. "OK. But I'm kinda tired, so maybe we won't go too far?"

"Just as far as you want, love," he said, and did a chin-chuck while wiggling his eyebrows at me in a way that let me know he was thinking about later. Tonight. Doing it. NAKED!!!! Eek!

OK. Not going into that now. Foreshadowing is *bad*. Back to the Rollerblading horror, and you just know it was a horror for me. We got set up with knee pads, elbow pads, wrist braces, helmets, and Rollerblades, and while Devon was off going potty, I ran back to the rental guys and had them show me how you stop on the stupid things. That meant I had to put them on, of course. For a while there I thought that maybe my ankles had done a miraculous strengthening thing. Devon came back and helped me sling Jack onto my back, giving him the eye as he said, "Looks a bit worse for wear, eh?"

"Yeah, well, he's been through a lot. I'm hoping to

clean him up and spackle the crack on his head before I have to turn him over to the school. I figure if I put a little pair of baby sunglasses on him, they might not notice that I lost his one eye until it's too late."

Devon didn't say anything to that, just held out his hand for me. I took a deep breath and crossed my fingers that my weak, pathetic ankles wouldn't give out before I went a couple of feet.

They lasted three blocks; then my right one suddenly caved in and went sideways. I jerked my hand away from Devon and one-footed my way over to the railing (we were on a road that curved alongside the Seine) like I wanted to admire the view.

"Oof!" I said as the railing slammed into my stomach.

"What's wrong?" Devon asked, stopping a few feet away from me.

"Nothing. Just . . . uh . . . the view and . . . um . . . I think I need to tighten the bindings."

See? I do listen to your advice. I figured you might have been right when you said that all I needed to do was to tighten the fastenings so the boot would support my ankles, and that's just what I did. Devon skated back and forth between all the people passing us by while I tightened. There were lots of families out, little kids zooming around like they had ankles of steel, and what was worse, old people who seemed to have no trouble. Gah!

"OK, I think that's better," I said as I straightened up. I wobbled only a little bit, which was pretty good considering that whole inner-ear, no-balance thing I have. And

148

yes, you're right, if you tighten the bindings really tight, it does seem to help. At least it was enough to keep my ankles from totally giving out.

"Erm . . . Emily?" Devon asked a few minutes later as I grabbed the back of his shirt for the third time. "You haven't rollerbladed much, have you?"

"Does it show?"

"No," he lied, which was really sweet, because I was holding on to him and letting him pull me along so I wouldn't have to chance moving my feet. "It just struck me that you might not have done this a lot."

"Oh. Well, as a matter of fact, I haven't. Not a lot. But it's fun; I'm really enjoying myself. A lot. Great big huge gobs of fun."

He pulled me around so I was next to him, slipping his arm around me (melt, melt, MELT!). "How about if we go a bit slower until you get your 'blading legs, then?"

I gave him my best smile, because he deserved it for being so thoughtful and not saying that I was the only person on the entire planet who didn't know how to Rollerblade. "Thanks, Devon. I'd like that."

Everything was fine until we turned off the nice next-to-the-river road. The skating route turned up a hill, which was OK, because that meant we really had to go slowly, but you know what's on the other side of going up a hill—coming down.

"Emily? Are you all right?" Devon called as we started down the hill. My skates started going faster and faster, and all of a sudden I realized two important facts: 1)

149

Devon wasn't next to me anymore; he was way behind me because I was evidently going warp three down the hill, and 2) I couldn't remember how the guy at the rental place said to stop if I was going too fast. Yeah, yeah, I know *you* know, but let me tell you, when you're streaking down a hill, more or less slaloming around people and kids and dogs, going so fast they're all just a blur, you tend to forget things. What do you call it when you're skiing? Schussing? That's what I was doing. I was a Rollerblading schusser fiend.

"Out of my way—I can't stop!" I yelled a warning as Jack and I rocketed past people. Ahead of me I could see the bottom of the hill, where the skating course made a left turn. I was absolutely positive I was not going to be able to make that turn. I'd probably pull a few Gs if I even tried (think of me looking like those astronauts training in the centrifuge with their faces all squished to the side by the force of gravity). It was awful, Dru, just awful. Zooming down that hill was just like the time when I was six and Bess and her evil friends put me on her bike that didn't have brakes and sent me down the long hill behind my house. You remember that? I hit a rock at the bottom and went flying. They called an ambulance to get me 'cause I was so skinned up. The only good thing about that was that Bess was grounded for months.

Yeah, so there I was, schussing down the Rue Brice-land, facing imminent death at the intersection where everyone but me was going to go left. I'd plow straight into the building that sat at the end of the street, and end up a big ol' Emily road pizza.

"No, I won't, either!" I swore to myself as I waved my arms around in hopes that I'd slow down. Behind me I could hear Devon yelling, but he sounded a long way off. "This is my birthday and I'm going to have sex later, and I refuse to kill myself before that. I'm just going to have to find some other way to stop."

I looked around for something to grab onto as I zoomed by, but I was going too fast. My eyes were watering, and it made it hard to see. Just as I was about to hit the bottom of the street, where everyone but me would be turning, I saw out of the corner of my eye a big black thing. I figured it was a light pole or something, so I lunged sideways and grabbed it.

Turns out it wasn't a light; it was a person. A tall, skinny person dressed totally in black. A Rollerblading goth— who knew they had them?

"*De l'air,*" the Rollergoth yelped as the force of my momentum swung me in an arc around him. "*Tu es fou?*" (Holly told me later that means he was asking me if I was an idiot.)

Then he went down. Fortunately, my arcing around him had slowed me down, and I let go of him just before he hit the ground. I spun over to the side of the road, where I grabbed a mailbox and clung to it.

Unfortunately, there was a group of six people who had linked arms and were skating right behind the Rollergoth. Two of the linked people tripped over him (he yelled a lot, I think someone rolled over his fingers), and they went down, pulling the other four with them. A few kids and a couple that were kissing while skating crashed into the six who were trying to get to their feet, and all of them fell, too. After that it was pretty much a big pileup. The bodies were lying all over the road, and people just couldn't stop in time to avoid crashing into them.

Devon was lucky. He was on the fringe, and landed on a big, burly guy. By the time he crawled off him and limped over to where I was still clinging to the mailbox, watching in horror as more and more bodies piled up, there was a pretty sizable crowd gathered to pick out the survivors.

Devon just looked at me for a minute, then cocked an eyebrow of rampant disbelief.

"I couldn't stop," I explained. "I . . . uh . . . forgot how you're supposed to stop when you're going fast. It's not really my fault; they should give you some sort of written instruction with the Rollerblades, don't you think?"

Devon smiled. OK, it wasn't his best smile, or even his second-best smile, but it was probably his fourteenth- or fifteenth-best smile, which is a lot considering the fact we were standing in front of a half-block-long scene of carnage with bodies writhing and screaming and swearing like mad. *At me.*

Devon just shook his head. "Emily, no matter what else you may be, you'll never be dull."

That's good, don't you think? Not being dull? I think it was a compliment.

After we walked back to the Rollerblading rental place (Devon thought we should get out of there before the first few people who crashed saw me, so we peeled off the Rollerblades and ran back up the hill), we hung around the river for a bit feeding the birds; then it was time to go to the canal boat place.

Crap, Madame wants to see me about something. Be back in a sec.

Hs and Ks
~Em

Subject: Back!
From: EmInParis@parisstudy.com
To: Dru@seattlegrrl.com
Date: 19 April 2004 12:58 pm

I wonder if Madame is related to Miss Horseface? She said the police were there asking if I had anything to do with the massive Rollerblading accident that happened yesterday afternoon. She held out a newspaper and pointed to an article with a picture of all the bodies lying around.

"Why do you think I had something to do with that?" I asked, blinking like mad because I didn't know what I was going to say.

She gave me the same look that Miss Horseface gives me whenever something goes wrong. "It is just a feeling I had. The police gave the description of a young American girl with curly blond hair and a baby in a backpack who is thought to have caused the"—she tipped the paper back to read from it—" 'greatest number of casualties Paris has seen since the German army claimed occupancy.' Is there something you wish to tell me?"

"No," I said, totally truthfully, because I really didn't want to tell her anything. It didn't do any good; she read me the riot act anyway about the importance of representing in a good light not just my fellow countrypeople, visitors to their fine country, but also the school, yadda yadda yadda. In the end she couldn't do anything but forbid me to go Rollerblading anymore, which was not an issue, because I wasn't about to try *that* again!

OK, so back to yesterday. Devon and I went to the canal boat place just as they were unchaining the gangplank, which meant we were the first on board. Go us!

The canal boat wasn't like boats back home—I mean, you couldn't water-ski from one. They're long and narrowish and have little flat roofs over the top. At the front is a bunch of chairs for people to sit on and look at stuff as you pass, and inside is a dining room, and more spots to sit (I guess if it's raining). It wasn't raining, so Devon and I got prime spots right up front.

About a half hour later the boat was filled up (mostly adults, although there were a couple of people our age from Denmark, and a few little kids). The boat took off, and Marcel, the tour guide (guy check: youngish, not very cute, wore chunky glasses), started telling us about the things we would see. "Our cruise starts with a parade of the most famous monuments in Paris: the Louvre, the Institute of France, the royal Sainte Chapelle, Notre Dame, and the Ile Saint-Louis."

"Haven't been there, seen it (looked boring), big and pretty from the outside, spent the night locked inside it, and has expensive shops," I whispered to Devon. He snickered and took my hand to do that lovely little thumb-swirly move on my wrist that always makes me melt.

"Following that, we arrive at the entrance to what has been called the most romantic street in all of Paris: the Canal Saint-Martin. It is three miles of jade-colored water that reflects old half-moon bridges, horse chestnut trees, and tender lovers embracing in the shadows."

"Ooooh," I said, going all shivery. "Doesn't that sound really fabu?"

"Romantic," Devon breathed in my ear. "A nice way to start the evening, eh?"

No, no, shrieked my insane mind. *He's not it! Don't do it!*

"Yeah," I said, because when have I ever let my mind control me? "Romantic."

To be honest, I spent the first hour of the boat trip worrying. I know, I know, you say I worry about every-thing, but honestly, Dru, if your mind went all wonky on you just when you needed it to make you look cool and sophisticated and all, you'd be worried too. So while the boat floated (these things won't win any speed awards) down the Seine and into a narrower river (the canal), I watched Devon. He was just as funny and adorable as he ever was, but something was . . . wrong.

I didn't have time to figure out what was going on before we were called in for the first sitting of dinner. There were more people than dining tables, so they did dinner in two sittings, and since we were in the first group, in we toddled. They handed us both menus; then Devon got a wine list, which is just so sexist, don't you think? On the other hand, it's très oilooc that France doesn't have a drinking age!

"Why can't women pick wine?" I asked as he eyed the list. "I mean, it's not like you have to have outdoor plumbing to figure out what wine goes with what, right? So why do they always give the guy the wine menu?"

"Good question," he said, his eyes laughing as he handed me the wine list. "Go ahead, use those brains I love. Pick us something good that'll go with dinner."

"What, you think I'm stupid or something? I can't pick a wine until I know what we're having." Sheesh! Did he think I never went to fancy dinner places with the p-units?

He grinned and read from the menu. "Let's see . . . how about the 'thin slices of red tuna with puree of black olives' as a starter?"

I shook my head. "Sorry, but I can't. Bess says the French don't use dolphin-safe tuna, and I couldn't eat a tuna that might have caused a dolphin to die."

"Ah. Well . . ." He looked back at his menu. It was in French, but also had English, so at least I wouldn't die of

156

embarassment by ordering something totally gacky, like fried hamster brains. (And no, I don't know that they eat fried hamster brains here, but let me tell you, some of the things they do eat are just as gross. That thing about snails is true—they eat them here like it's nothing! SNAILS!!! What will they think of next, stew of slugs? Puree of potato bug? Worm casserole? Gack overtime!)

"How about the 'nature melon from Cavaillon with San Daniele ham'?"

"Ham!" I wrinkled my nose.

"Oh, that's right, you're off ham."

"I don't eat pigs, cows, or sheep," I said righteously. "They're mammals, warm-blooded like us. I couldn't eat my fellow mammal. It wouldn't be right. Except for McDonald's, of course, but that doesn't count."

Devon pursed his lips as he eyed the menu. "How about this? 'Tartare of crab meat with herbs'—you like crab, don't you?"

"I'm from Seattle; of course I like crab. Herbed crab sounds OK." I looked down at the wine list. "Um. How many wines will we be needing, do you think?"

"One for every course is traditional, but"—Devon gave me a weird look—"I think we'll just have one with the entrée."

"Oh. OK. So what are you going to have?"

"I think I'll go with the *filet de boeuf Wellington*. What looks good to you?"

"The *coq au vin*. It says it's chicken marinated and cooked in red wine, with mushrooms and bacon.

Nummy. OK, so let's see, that's one chicken and one *boeuf,* so . . . um . . . uh . . ."

"Want me to help?" Devon asked, holding out his hand for the wine list.

"No! I can do this. It's my birthday. Um . . ." OK, to be honest, I didn't know what I was looking for. All the wines names were in French, and even if they weren't, I had a horrible feeling that I wouldn't know one from the other. They had two listed as sweet, though, and I thought that sounded good. Maybe it would be like a wine cooler. Those margarita ones we had that time your mom was in Denver were pretty cool. "Let's go with this one. It was made in 2000, which was a fabu year. Its name is Denechaud."

Devon nodded and gave our order when the waiter came by. Then we acted really cool and sipped our Cokes and had bread and stuff until the crab appetizer came.

"What's this?" I asked when the waiter set down a plate of what looked like cat barf. It was all chopped-up and ugly, with bits of green flecks, and little sprigs of parsley artistically arranged around the edges of the cat barf.

"It's the crab tartare."

I made squinty eyes at it. "That's crab? It doesn't look like any crab I've seen. And where's the tartar sauce?"

Devon scooped up a wad of cat barf on one of the tiny little round crackers that came in a bowl with the barf. "It's crab tartare, Emily. There's no tartar sauce."

I blinked at him a couple of times.

"Tartare means minced raw meat, so herbed crab tartare is minced raw crab with herbs. It's pretty good."

"Raw!" I watched as he ate another cracker of barf. "EW! Ew, ew, ew! I'm not eating raw crab! That's just gross! You'll probably get worms or something!"

"It's perfectly safe; people eat it all the time. Try some." He tried to shove a bit of barf on cracker into my mouth. I clamped my teeth shut and did the nostril-flare thing that Brother is so good at doing. "No . . . raw . . . crab . . ." I hissed through my clenched teeth.

"Want me to order something else?"

"No," I said, relaxing a bit as he popped another cracker into his mouth. "I'll be fine with just dinner."

That's what I thought, anyway, but after they took the crab barf away and gave us salads (which were normal, thank God), they brought the main part of dinner. Everything was copacetic until I looked down to see my dinner. It was chicken, all right, the leg and thigh piece of a chicken (not cut apart), covered in a brown sauce with bits of mushrooms and bacon, but OHMIGOD, Dru, they left the chicken's foot on! Claws and all, it was right there on my plate, next to a poof of potatoes. And the claws had TOENAILS! EEEEK! Chicken toenails on my plate!

"Is something wrong?" Devon asked as I stared in horror at the atrocity.

How on earth was I going to eat something that still had its toenails attached? "Uh . . . no. Fine. It's fine."

I took a deep breath and tried to get a grip. I was seventeen, on a romantic canal boat tour with my boyfriend, and we were having an elegant dinner with wine. I had already made a scene about the crab/cat barf; I wasn't going to make another about the fact that someone forgot to cut off the chicken's foot before they cooked it.

EW! Icky thought! They cooked the foot and all with the rest of the stuff! The mushrooms could have TOUCHED CLAW! Eeeeeeeeeeeeeeeeeeeew!

"Em?" Devon asked, looking up from his perfectly normal slab of cow.

"Sorry, just thinking. Num. Chicken." I picked up my fork and stabbed it into the chicken thigh, but the sight of that claw just ruined my appetite, so I started to pull my fork back, figuring I'd eat the potatoes, but somehow the fork got stuck on the chicken and I ended up holding a chicken thigh and leg in midair over my plate.

Devon caught me trying to shake it off my fork. He raised his eyebrows.

"Look," I said, trying to laugh it off. "It walks!" I made the chicken leg walk around the plate on its foot. "Cute, huh?"

Devon looked at me like I had claws coming out the top of my head. "Cute."

In the end I buried the claw part in the potatoes so I wouldn't have to see it, and managed to eat enough of the chicken thigh to make Devon happy.

The rest of the dinner was OK, although the wine wasn't very good. It was awfully sweet, but not at all like a wine cooler. I didn't drink all of mine, and I noticed

Devon didn't drink much of his, either, although he didn't say anything. Maybe the same person who didn't cut off the chicken's foot messed up the wines, too.

After dinner we went back out to the seats to watch the now-dark Paris float by. Devon put his arm around me in a majorly cool move, and I felt all Emily the Seductress, except just as I was thinking that I might want to indicate to Devon that it would be OK if he wanted to kiss me, my brain went wonky again and started saying stupid stuff about not ruining a perfectly good friendship by trying to do something I didn't want to do, which really didn't make sense, because I did want to do it; I really did. It was my birthday, and it was time. I had a boyfriend. I was an adult. I was going to do it if it killed me.

"What's the matter, love?" Devon asked at one point as we were floating under a cool arched bridge, his nummy blue eyes all scrunched up as he frowned at me. "You've been quiet most of the evening. You're not seasick, are you?"

All of a sudden my stomach gave a chicken-clawed lurch. He would have to mention being seasick! Blech.

"Maybe just a little," I said, wishing I could turn off my brain. As soon as he said the magic words my stomach rolled around and did a couple of backflips, and all I could think of was the cook throwing the raw chicken leg with claw into a pan and cooking it.

"There are no waves on a canal, Emily, so there's nothing to make you seasick. It's all in your mind. You just need to get your sea legs, and then you'll feel better.

Come on; we'll walk to the back of the boat. Moving around will help you regain your balance."

Just as we made it to the back of the boat, we hit the tunnel. There's a mile and a half of it—Marcel said it was the underground vault of what used to be the Bastille. Whatever it was, it was dark, and I clutched the railing of the boat while my stomach tried to decide whether or not it was going to hang on to the bit of dinner I'd managed to eat.

"Emily?" Devon's voice came out of the blackness. "Where are you, love?"

"Right here. I think I'm going to ralph."

"Poor Em. Hang on; keep talking and I'll find you."

We drifted into a section of the tunnel that had lights, and suddenly Devon was there, all sweet and wonderful, and so gorgeous he made my tongue swell up in my mouth when I thought about him being my exclusive BF.

"You look awful. Close your eyes and take a deep breath." He put both his arms around me really gently, like I was made of glass or something.

I closed my eyes, but I clenched my teeth together as I did. After all, I'd already barfed on the guy once since we'd known each other; I wasn't going to do it again. There's just nothing like ralphing to ruin an evening of romance.

A few minutes later the boat cleared the tunnel, and we were back out into the night lights of Paris. I was feeling better, what with leaning against Devon and breathing and stuff, so I figured that since we were alone in the back of the boat, now would be the time to kiss him.

"Em," Devon murmured as I turned in his arms to face him.

"Devon," I whispered against his lips just as I was going to really plant one on him.

"WAAAAAAAAAAAAAAAAH!" said Jack.

"Bloody hell!" Devon jumped when Jack went off (he is very loud). "What timing that doll has."

"Sorry," I said, swinging the backpack off so I could pull Jack out. "It won't take me long, I'm su— OH, NO!"

Somehow—and I swear I fastened Jack into the backpack like I normally do—somehow he got loose, and when I swung the backpack around he went flying out of it. Right over the edge of the railing and into the canal.

"OHMIGOD!" I yelled just as a woman behind me screamed bloody murder.

"Le bébé! Le bébé!"

Devon told me later that she had just walked out of the dining room and thought that Jack was a real baby, which explains the fact that she just about had a heart attack right then and there. Just like me. "OHMIGOD, Devon, what am I going to do?" I asked as Jack bobbed off slowly, getting farther and farther from the boat. He was still crying, but the cries were kind of muffled by the water. "This is going to show up as abuse, I just know it is, and I'll fail the stupid class, and won't make it to Harvard, and my WHOLE ENTIRE LIFE will be ruined!"

Devon sighed and headed for the front of the boat.

"I'll see if they have a boat hook I can use to grab him."

The screaming lady started jumping up and down while pointing over the edge of the boat. A whole bunch more people came out to see what was up.

"It's OK; it's just a fake baby," I told them. "My boyfriend is going to get a boat hook."

Evidently no one spoke English (or couldn't hear me over the screaming woman's yells—she must have been an opera singer or something, because I swear she could have pierced eardrums with her screams), because they all got excited with her and started screaming and pointing at where Jack was now floating upside down.

"Poop!" I said as I watched him. Devon was nowhere in sight. Although the boat was going slowly, it wasn't going that slowly, and if Devon didn't show up in the next few seconds, I knew I was going to have to go get Jack myself.

That's what happened, of course. When does anything ever go right in my life? Everyone was still jumping around, pointing and yelling. Screaming Woman was hauling on the arm of some bald guy, dragging him over to the railing as I peeled off my jacket and set my purse down with the jacket over it. Behind everyone, at the far end of the boat, a guy in a uniform came running, but he didn't have a boat hook or anything that could grab Jack.

"Oh, great, oh, just effing great. I can hear Miss Horseface now going on and on about Jack being my responsibility. Fine. Now I have to go save him. I'm *never* having kids!" I climbed onto the bench that curved around the rear of the boat, grabbed my nose (you know how I always get water up my nose when I dive), and jumped in.

OK, two things about canal water in France: in April it's really, really cold, and it stinks. A lot.

"Hold on, Jack; I'm coming," I yelled as I tried to catch my breath, although why I yelled to him, I have no idea; it just seemed like the thing to do. The water was icy cold, and I swear I went into instant hypothermia, but I could see Jack bobbing a few yards away from me. I started swimming toward him.

The yelling and screaming on the boat got even louder, and then there were a couple of big splashes. I looked over my shoulder and saw the bald guy that Screaming Woman was hauling around swimming toward me, a grim look on his face. The second splash was the boat guy in uniform. He was also swimming toward me, saying something that I didn't understand because my survival French doesn't include "Things to Say in a Canal When People Are Trying to Save Your Fake Baby."

"It's OK, he's fake!" I yelled over my shoulder as I swam toward Jack, trying really hard to ignore both the smell of the water and the fact that my entire body had turned to ice.

The boat guy must have been on a swim team, like you, 'cause he made it to me just as I reached Jack. I grabbed Jack by one arm, and he grabbed the other. He said something urgent-sounding.

"*Fakez-vous*," I said, my teeth chattering like mad. "It's not a real baby. Doll! See? I have a key for him."

He said something else and pulled Jack toward him, but I wasn't going to let him have him. I had to get Jack's key into his back pronto or the whole horrible time with him would be ruined.

Unfortunately, the boat guy didn't understand me. Also unfortunately, he was holding on to Jack's bad arm, the one the *clochard* had yanked out of its socket.

This time the arm came off altogether.

The boat guy had the most amazed look on his face as he floated there in the middle of the canal treading water, holding Jack's arm in his hand. The people on the boat (which had stopped) went silent for a moment; then Screaming Woman shrieked, and fainted dead away.

"Oh, *thank you* so very much," I said kinda snappily, which I admit wasn't nice of me, because Boat Guy was trying to help me, but honestly, he pulled Jack's arm off! How was I going to explain *that?* I snatched the arm back and stuck my key into Jack's back, praying I had enough time to get back to the boat and get his bottle in him before the computer chip registered that he had cried too long without attention. Boat Guy kind of made a gulping sound, then started saying things that I just knew weren't at all nice. By that time the captain was standing at the back next to Devon.

"I got him!" I yelled to Devon, and held Jack up so he could see him. He gave me a thumbs-up, then went around to the side to where they had lowered a rope ladder thingy over the side so we could climb back in. Boat Guy (who was still swearing) and I both passed Bald Guy, which would be really funny except it was nice and all of Bald Guy to jump into the water just because he thought my baby was drowning. So I thanked him through my chattering teeth as I swam by him. He didn't say much, just kind of glared at me. I don't suppose I blame him, but sheesh! I *was* being polite!

The rest of the boat ride kind of sucked after that. I was too cold to even think of kissing Devon and enjoying a romantic voyage, so after I went into the bathroom and put on a pair of jeans and a sweater that belonged to Boat Guy, Devon took the opportunity the captain offered us of getting off the boat early.

"You'd think I was cursed or something," I told Devon as we got out of a taxi in front of his hotel. "Who else do you know who goes to Paris for two weeks to learn French and ends up with a fake baby, getting locked in Notre Dame, causing a bunch of people to get hurt while Rollerblading, and having to jump into a canal to rescue a doll?"

"That's what I like about you," Devon said as we walked to the elevator. He was carrying a plastic bag that had my wet clothes in it. I was still in Boat Guy's extra clothes (I had seen Devon slipping the guy some euros, so I guess they were mine now, although the jeans were grotty and too big, and the sweater had weird armpit stains on it), and I had Jack's extra arm stuffed into my purse, which thankfully no *gamins* had gotten to while I was in the canal.

Course, thinking about it, I don't think there were any *gamins* on the boat. I mean, they wouldn't want to shell over a ton of money to pick pockets, would they?

Devon just looked at me. We got into the elevator with a couple of fancy old people—you know, the kind where the guy has a full suit and tie, and not a lot of hair, which is cut really short, and the lady has that big poofy hair that looks like it's been teased and sprayed to death, and what my Mom calls "discreet" makeup, which we both know means "really needs to take a peek at *Vogue* or *Cosmo* to get a clue"—anyway, there was this old couple who wrinkled up their noses at me.

"It's my clothes; they stink. I had to dive into the canal to save Jack." I took out Jack's arm and waved it at them. The woman's eyes opened up really wide. "He's fake, just in case you're thinking he's real. But that's why I smell, although it's not really me that smells; it's my clothes. I'm not like a *clochard* or anything. I take a shower every morning."

"Emily," Devon said, his lips doing a funny twitch thing.

"Yeah?"

"I don't think they understand you."

I looked at the couple. They avoided meeting my eyes. "Oh. Sorry. Never *mindez-moi.*"

It hit me then as we were zooming up to the twelfth floor (the oldsters got off on the seventh) that there I was, with Devon, alone, together in the elevator of a Paris hotel, and we were going to his hotel room—alone, together!!!—to have sex.

OHMIGOD!!!

Devon was saying something about going to see the Catacombs tomorrow as we got off on his floor. "I don't know, maybe we should see if they have some sort of traveler's insurance, Em. I hate to think of how much it'll cost your father if you end up bringing the whole of the Catacombs down."

I looked at him as he dug his room key out of his pocket. He was Devon. We were going to his room. To have sex. The two of us. Together. NAKED. Where his body was going to . . . you know, and my body would be there, too, and they would do things. Together. Oh, my God. OHMIGOD.

"Emily?" Devon opened the door to his room and looked back at me.

"*OHMIGOD!*" I yelled, and started hyperventilating. My stomach wadded up into a tiny little knot. I think I even weaved where I stood, and you know me, I *never* weave!

Devon swore under his breath and pulled me into the room, closing the door behind us. It clanged shut just like it was a metal jail cell door.

I felt all weird, like I was someone else, like I was in one of those artsy movies that Bess likes to see, you know, the ones with dwarfs with pink hair, and horses walking through the middle of a room, and people who talk to artichokes, and weirdo stuff like that.

"Em, it's just me. Calm down."

He stood there, all guyish. He was a guy. He had guy parts. Naked guy parts. He had naked guy parts under his clothes, and I had told him that I wanted to frolic with those naked guy parts, and that he could see my girl parts, and OHMIGOD, what was I going to do, because I suddenly realized that the part of my mind that I had thought was insane really wasn't. Mom was always going on about sex being boring if it wasn't done with someone really special, and although I loved Devon, right at that moment I realized that I loved him like a really good friend and not like a guy whose thingy I wanted to come visiting all my inner parts.

"Emily?"

I just stood there clutching Jack's arm and my purse and my book bag filled to the rim with condoms and a slinky negligee and lacy undies, and my stinky bag of wet clothes, and I looked into Devon's gorgeous blue eyes as he hovered in front of me, a worried expression on his face. He was so nummy, so nice, and so thoughtful, and he didn't treat me like he just wanted one thing. He really cared about me. He liked my being better at math than him, and he gave me a ring and came to Paris so we could be together. He was perfect. PERFECT! He was everything I'd ever wanted in a BF, and I knew I was the stupidest stupid, stupid, idiot boob who ever lived, because there he was all hottalicious and gorgeous and he was mine!

And I was going to have to tell him that I didn't want to have sex with him.

Now, I know what you're thinking. You're thinking I freaked out on him, aren't you? You're thinking that I lost it big-time, just started screaming and wigging out royally, but I didn't. I kept telling myself that I was seventeen. I was an adult. I could handle this situation just like Bess or someone else who has a lot of cool.

"Gack!" I said, and barfed on his shoes.

"Please," I said to the inside of Devon's toilet a couple of minutes later, "just let me drown here. You don't have to tell my parents anything. They'll understand. Honest."

"Don't be ridiculous. You're just still a bit seasick. Or it's the excitement of having to swim in the canal."

"This is the second time I've barfed on you," I wailed to the toilet, then decided my barfing spree was over. I lifted my head and took the glass of water he held out, rinsed, and spit into the toilet. "I'm so sorry, Devon. It's like you're some sort of horrible vomit magnet around me. Obviously I'm never going to be able to see you again, because I'm so embarassed I'm going to die in the next couple of minutes, but I want you to know how much I like you and love you and that you're really nice and all."

He laughed and stood up, wetting a washcloth before handing it to me. I slumped back against the bathtub, grimaced, then hauled Jack and his backpack off my back so I could sit without squishing him. "Thank you, but you're not going to die. Here, wash your face; you'll feel better. You can use my toothbrush if you like."

"I have my own," I said sadly, then realized what I said. I had my own because I was expecting to spend the night with him after we had done it.

"Eek," I whispered, too exhausted to even work up a good squeal, as Devon closed the bathroom door. I sat there for a while crying—just a little bit, though, because I always think it's so sad to cry in a bathroom where you can see yourself crying. It might be OK if you can cry without your eyes going all red and puffy, and your nose running, and your cheeks going blotchy, but since all of that happens when I cry, the last thing I wanted was to see it happening.

Jack went off again. I think the water did something to his insides, because his cry doesn't sound quite like a baby's cry anymore, it sounds more like . . . hmmm . . . you remember that old fat wiener dog your grandma had, the one whose thingy dragged on the ground when he walked? You remember how it couldn't bark anymore, but it made kind of a funny coughing sound? Well, that's sort of what Jack's cry was like. It was more wiener-dog cough than cry.

I pulled him out of his backpack and dug out the bottle, stuffing it in his mouth as I put the key in his back, then sat there feeding him until Devon came in.

"You all right? Oh. Jack again, huh?"

"Yeah. Sometimes he doesn't wait long before he wants attention."

Devon hoisted himself up onto the bathroom counter

and frowned. "Doesn't sound like he's any better for his dip into the Canal Saint-Martin."

"I know." I looked down at Jack as he drank his water. He really was in bad shape, what with the one eye missing, and the crack on his head (which seemed to get worse after the canal thing), and the one arm, and the blue mouth and butt and stuff. "I don't see how Horseface can say I neglected him, though. I jumped into the canal for him! I could have drowned or something."

"I'm sure she won't think that."

"You never know with her," I said darkly. We sat there for a few minutes not saying anything. I did a little lip gnawing, wondering how I was going to tell Devon that I'd changed my mind about doing the big S with him.

I know, I know, it was crazy even thinking it, but Dru, something didn't feel right, and I realized that what Mom said was true (I know, who'd have thought?!?)—I wanted to do it, but not with Devon. I mean, I did, but . . . I didn't. If that makes sense. Oh, I know it doesn't; even I didn't understand it. All I knew was that although he was gorgeous and me made me drool, and he was nice and adorable and everything, I didn't want to do it.

"You don't want to go to bed with me, do you?" Devon asked, just like he was reading my mind, his face carefully blank.

I really wanted to cry then, but I kept telling myself that I was seventeen now, and I couldn't act like a big old baby.

"I want to, I really do, but I . . ." I waved my hand around like I thought that would help.

It didn't.

"But you what? Don't fancy me?"

"No, of course I do, I fancy you a lot."

"Good," Devon said, and stood up to peel his shirt off. My eyes bugged out as I looked at his bare chest. *Devon's bare chest!* Right there in front of me! "Because I've fancied you ever since I met you."

He pulled his shoes and socks off.

"Gark," I said, and looked at his feet. His *naked* feet.

"And I thought you felt the same way." He undid his belt. I felt my jaw hit my knees as I realized he was going to take off all his clothes right then and there.

"Mmmfalg," was the only thing I could think of to say, and yes, I'm aware that it doesn't mean anything in any known human language. It probably translates as "OMG, he's getting naked!" in Klingon or something, though.

"And since you said you wanted to do this on your birthday, well, the least I can do is oblige you," he said, his hand on the top button of his jeans.

All that stood between me and his thingy was his hand on his button. Well, OK, not literally, because he was probably wearing underwear (guys don't go around not wearing undies, do they? I mean, wouldn't they get stuck in their zippers and stuff if they didn't?), and he was across the room from me, so there was air between us, but you know what I mean. All that stood between me and *the moment* was his hand on his button. If I let him

174

unbutton it, I would have to do it with him. I would be too embarassed to back out after seeing him naked, because then he'd think it was something to do with him, and not me, and it *was* me. I'm sure it was me. So if I didn't stop him, I'd have to do it, even though my stomach was knotting up again just thinking about getting naked and being in the same bed together with all our parts touching each other.

I looked up at Devon, looked into his really nice blue eyes, and thought about how wonderful he was, and how nice he made me feel, and how much I enjoyed being with him. How much I loved him.

"No," I said as his fingers slid the button of his jeans through the buttonhole. "I changed my mind. If it's not that big a deal to you, I think I'd better go back home. I don't want Holly to get into trouble for me. Not again. And . . . and I don't think it's fair to you, to make you . . . *you know* . . . when I don't really want to. You'd notice, wouldn't you? That I didn't want to? And then you'd feel bad, like you did something wrong?"

"Yes," Devon said, his fingers still on his button. "I'd notice."

I didn't say anything else, because all I wanted to do was to curl up in bed and have a really good cry, but I couldn't because I was an adult and Devon was my BF, and I didn't want to make him feel bad because I had chickened out of having sex.

His fingers rebuttoned the button. He even laughed a little laugh, although it was kind of an odd laugh, like it was stretched really thin. "And I'm glad you told me now, because I would have figured it was something I was doing. Emily—"

I sniffled just a little as he squatted down in front of me, trying not to notice that he still had naked feet, and a bare chest, and his tat of the dragon curling around his arm, and all the rest of him right there in front of me.

"Emily, you know I'm not going to force you to do anything you don't want to do."

"I'd have to hit you if you did," I sniffed, and accepted the wad of toilet paper he handed me. I did a little nose blow, hoping I wasn't grossing him out with thoughts of snot and all. "Mom and Bess and I went to a self-defense class last year. I know how to gouge someone's eyes out with car keys. I like your eyes, Devon. They're pretty, and I don't want to have to gouge them out."

He put both his hands on my knees as he laughed, this time the laugh making it up to his eyes. "That's my girl. As I said, I'll never force you, but are you sure? This is the perfect opportunity to have time to ourselves without your parents being on our backs."

"I'm sure," I said, pulling the bottle out of Jack's mouth. He was quiet, so I figured he was happy—that or the canal water had killed his insides. I was still feeling really woobidy around the tummy region, but a bit better in the brain department. "I'm sorry. I know you were looking forward to . . . *it*."

He laughed again, but this time made a face as he did, like something was hurting him. "I wouldn't be a guy if

I wasn't looking forward to it. But I suppose it won't kill me to wait a bit longer for you."

"No," I said, completely surprised by what my mouth was saying. I didn't remember agreeing that it could say anything else other than, *No, thank you, I don't want to have sex now*. "No, I'm not going to want to do it later, either. In fact—" I clapped my hand over my mouth. What was I doing? What was my brain telling my mouth to say? I didn't tell it to say those things!

I swear to God, Dru, I think aliens took over my body, because before I could slap a second hand over the first, my fingers spread and my mouth said, "I don't think we should date anymore. I like you a lot, Devon—I love you—but only like a friend, not like a boyfriend."

See what I mean? Aliens. There's just no other reason for my mouth to be saying those words. I mean, just because I didn't want to have sex with him didn't mean I had to dump him as a BF, right?

Devon looked at me without saying anything for a minute; then he grimaced. "Ow. I never thought having a bird tell me no would hurt, but I was wrong."

"Oh, Devon," I said, getting to my feet so I could hold his hands. "That's why it's better if we break up. What you want out of a relationship is not what I want."

It took me a couple of seconds before I realized what the aliens were making me say, and then I slapped both hands over my mouth. "I'm sorry," I mumbled behind my fingers, wondering if there was somewhere I could get some foil so I could make a foil hat to keep the alien's mind rays out of my head. "I don't know what I'm saying. Just ignore me. I'm having some sort of insane moment. I'm sure it'll pass."

"Are you?" Devon did his cute head tip, the one that always melts my heart, only this time my heart didn't melt. "I'm not so sure that you're not right. Maybe it is a bit too much for you."

I shook my head. "Yes, you're right, it's too much. Eek! What am I saying? Ignore me! Ignore my mouth! It's not saying what I want it to say!"

Devon laughed and pulled me into another one of his specialty hottie-guy hugs. "Emily Williams, I've always said you're a brainy bird, and you've just proven it again." He gave me a little kiss, just a tiny one, a friendly sort of a kiss you would give a girl who used to be your girlfriend but who wasn't going to do it with you. "Stop looking like your dog just died. It's all right."

"You hate me," I sniffled, totally giving in and going drama queen. "And I don't blame you. I know guys have a name for girls who make them think they want to do it, then don't. I'm not naïve."

"Yes, you are, but that's one of your charms," Devon said with a really nice smile. He tucked a bit of hair behind my ear before his hands settled onto my shoulders. "Ah, Em. I had a feeling it wasn't going to work. It's Fang you really want, isn't it?"

"Fang?" I gasped, totally shocked. "Fang? You think I want *Fang* as a boyfriend?"

"He wants you," Devon said, watching me carefully.

"I assumed that was what was holding you back with me."

"No," I said, stepping back. Have you ever! Fang! "I like Fang, and I miss him and everything, but not as a boyfriend. He's . . . he's Fang! And you're wrong about him; he doesn't like me that way. He told me last year he thought I was immature."

Devon shrugged. "Whatever he told you, he's had it for you for a long time. We both have, although it's a bit different with Fang. He's not a player."

"And you are," I said, still stunned. Fang!

Devon gave me one of his shoelace-melting grins. "Yeah, well, you are who you are. I thought Fang'd make his move in Scotland, but he said he wanted to wait, so I decided to see how things stood with you."

"Fang?" I asked, trying to take in the whole idea. Fang had a crush on me? ME???

"You could at least look a little unhappy over breaking up with me," Devon said as I grabbed Jack and his stuff and walked out of the bathroom.

"Fang likes me that way? *The cow!*"

"You know, maybe cry just a little bit. Or tell me how much you love me, and how you'll always be my friend, and never forget our time together."

"I have to tell Holly!" I said, gathering up my purse and jacket. "This is amazing! *Fang!* Bess is going to have kittens. She said all along Fang was that way about me."

"You could write me a really nice note, too, the kind girls write with pink pens and little hearts dotting the Is."

"This changes everything," I said as I opened the door. "Fang. I never would have guessed."

"Night, Emily," Devon said in a little, itty-bitty voice as he stood in the middle of his room.

"Hmm? Oh, night." I started to close the door, let it get so it almost clicked shut, then opened it again. "You great big idiot! Did you really think I am the kind of girl who would just walk out of here and leave you?"

The look on his face said it all. I set my stuff down and ran across the room, throwing myself into his arms (manly and all that). "Such a silly! Like I'd do that to you."

He laughed and tightened his arms around me, and swung me around the room.

"Oorf," I said, feeling a bit barfy still.

"Sorry."

" 'S OK. But you deserved to be punished for thinking I'd just walk out on you. I might not want to have sex with you, and I think it's probably for the best if we break it off—nicely, of course—but I still do like you a lot, Devon. You're one of my best friends!"

He made that face that guys do when they are embarrassed when you tell them nice stuff. I pinched his arm and said, "After all, I wouldn't barf on just anyone!"

He took me home in a taxi later, and even though it was after curfew, I made it in without getting into trouble. Holly was surprised to see us, but I whispered to her that I'd explain it all later.

Whew! My fingers are tired, and I'm hungry, so I'm going to go see what's for lunch. Now you know what happened to me, tell me everything that's going on there. What name are you using now? Spill all! I miss your gossip, girl!

Hugs and kisses,
~Still just Em

Subject: Re: Wait just one d*mned second!
From: EmInParis@parisstudy.com
To: Dru@seattlegrrl.com
Date: 20 April 2004 7:33 am

> *Look what you made me do, I swore in e-mail! Father*
> *Sinclair is going to have a hissy at confession!*

Hey, I am not my sister's keeper!
   No, I'm not quite sure what that means, but it was something I heard on TV. I think. Anyway, I'm not responsible for your potty fingers in e-mail. Besides, by now FS has heard it all from you. A little swearing in e-mail isn't nearly as bad as that time you tried to seduce Vance the Wonder Weasel. Heh heh heh.

> *All right, let's start at the beginning. You fell in a canal.*

No, I jumped in a canal; there's a difference.

> *You told Devon, your BF of three months—that's*
> *THREE MONTHS—the guy who gave you a really*

> expensive ring, the guy who makes you drool
> whenever you see him, the guy you go on and on and
> on about until I swear my brain is going to explode out
> my ears, you told that guy that you not only didn't
> want to get busy with him, but that you DON'T EVEN
> WANT HIM AS A BF?

Right.

> You don't even sound like you're upset or anything!
> Where's your whiny e-mails? Where's the sniveling and
> humongo pity party? Where's the gazillion e-mails to
> me asking me if I think you did the right thing, and
> what would I do in your place, and whether or not
> Devon really deserved you, and how you were a
> horrible GF and turning him free was so noble of you,
> and you really should be Saint Emily, blah blah blah?

You know, if you weren't my best friend, I'd take . . .
um . . . what's that word . . . it starts with a U . . . sec,
there's a dictionary over there . . . umbrage, that's it, I'd
take umbrage with you! Because I don't do all that. I
might ask your advice every once in a while, but that's
only because you're my friend and I want you to know
how much I miss you.

   And I really should be Saint Emily, you know.

> That's just not like you, Em!

I *am* upset. I *was* upset. I probably will be upset tomorrow. But not *upset* upset, you know? I mean, I hurt inside when I think about Devon not being my BF, but it's not a horrible hurt; it's kind of a good hurt, like I'm doing something right. And I'm sad, too, because I really wanted to do it with him, but I *don't* want to more. If that makes sense.

OHMIGOD, you don't think I'm turning into my mother, do you? The cow! I am! She always told me she was turning into her mother; I bet she passed something on to me genetically and now I'm turning into her. Aaaaaaaaack!

OK, I'm back. I had to go take a walk 'cause I was hyperventilating again. Anyhoo, I am upset; I'm just not crying-and-wanting-to-die upset. I don't know, maybe this is what the 'rents are always saying is growing up— the kind of achey, "doing what you know is right even though you really don't want to do it" feeling. If so, I'd like to skip right over the rest of it and go straight into fun twenty-something years, 'K?

> *And what's with the thing with Fang? What are you*
> *going to do about that?*

Nothing. What am I supposed to do, go home and say, "Oh, hey, Fang, I hear you have the hots for me; wanna do the nasty?" I mean, get real! If Fang truly wants to be my BF—and that's a big if, because despite what Devon and Bess say, I haven't seen any BF signs from Fang—

then I'll think about it. What if Devon is wrong? What if he was right, but Fang has changed his mind about me? What if I don't feel the same way about him that he feels about me? I like him so much, I really don't want to ruin anything.

Gah! I hate my life! Why can't anything be easy?

> *My name du jour (that's French!) is Ariadne. Yeah,*
> *yeah, I know that's really your name because you had*
> *a stuffed elephant named Ariadne, but I like it. I think*
> *I look like an Ariadne. What do you think?*

I think you can be whoever you want to be. And you know what? So can I.

Gotta run. Devon is coming by to take Holly and me and the GTs to the Catacombs. Devon had to swear to Madame that he wouldn't let me touch anything in order for me to go, which is just silly. I mean, what can happen in a big underground cave with a bunch of bones?

Étreintes et baisers (that's French for hugs and kisses, and is your phrase for the day),
~Em

Subject: Accidents can happen . . . a lot!
From: EmInParis@partisstudy.com
To: Akrigon@gobottle.co.uk
Date: 20 April 2004 7:38 am

Hi Mr. Krigon. Can you tell me how much those Luv-MyBaby dolls cost? Mine is . . . uh . . . missing some bits. And it coughs instead of cries. I think the computer in it crashed. That's not going to affect my grade, right? After all, it's not like I did anything *wrong* to it. It's just a software glitch. I think.

    Emily

Subject: Re: Is everything all right?
From: EmInParis@parisstudy.com
To: Fbaxter@oxfordshire.agricoll.co.uk
Date: 21 April 2004 2:40 pm

Fbaxter wrote:
> *That was a very strange e-mail you sent me this*
> *morning. I don't think I've ever had one that just said*
> *"Um." Is something wrong there? Are you OK? You*
> *didn't get stuck in another cathedral, did you? If you*
> *need any help, let me know. You know I'm always*
> *here for you.*

Um. I mean . . . er . . . no. Everything is . . . uh . . . fine. Yeah. Fine. Thanks, though, that's sweet of you. To offer your help. To me. It's . . . nice. Oh, poop, never mind, just ignore me; I don't know what I'm saying. I've recently discovered that my brain has gone insane, and I no longer have control over it.

Big smoochy . . . hugs.

GAH!

Emily

P.S. That story that was on CNN about the American who was caught trying to smuggle out a complete skeleton from the Catacombs? It wasn't me.

P.P.S. Just in case you wondered.

P.P.P.S. I'm not going anywhere with the GTs ever again, though. They're just nothing but trouble!

P.P.P.P.S. I'll be home on Saturday, in case you want to . . . uh . . . doesn't matter. Never mind.

P^5.S. Miss you.

Turn the page for a special sneak
preview of Emily's adventures in . . .

the taming
of the dru

Coming in September!

Subject: Sooooooo coolio!
From: Emmers@britsahoy.co.uk
To: Dru@seattlegrrl.com
Date: 1 August 2004 10:23 pm

Hey, chicky, I'm back from the trip to London. Ahmed at the Tongue and Groove club says hi. (Yeah, Holly's brother, Peter, got us into the club, which is majorly coolio, let me tell you!) Anyhoo, when I got home last night, Brother was all "I've got a secret." You know how I hate it when he does that. Why can't I have a normal father? One that doesn't play with medieval torture devices?

"Your secret is that you get turned on by thumbscrews?" I asked, watching with more than a little concern as Brother toyed with a reproduction thumbscrew. (One of his fellow professors at Oxford has come up with a line of torture toys based on the originals. Brother says it'll make millions. I say why didn't he think of that so *we* could have millions?)

"No, of course not," he said, his unibrow all scrunched up into a frown.

"Because if you and Mom are getting into kinky stuff, I don't want to know about it," I warned. "I'm only just managing to forget that horrible thing that Mom said to me last year."

His unibrow furrowed even more. "What horrible thing?"

"That you guys have a healthy sex life. Bleh."

Brother sighed and looked upward for a couple of seconds, like he was praying or something. "Emily, why does every conversation I have with you end up being about sex?"

"Because you're obsessed with it," I said gently, and even patted him on the arm so he wouldn't think I hated him for it. "But that's OK, I've learned to live with it."

His hand ruffled through his hair, which probably would have formed his usual hair horn, but did I tell you he got his hair cut last week? He couldn't get in to his regular guy, so he went to a new one, Mr. Manny, who buzzed his hair instead of doing the old-guy 'do, so now Brother looks kind of like Boris Karloff. With bulgy pug eyes. "That's it; I give up. I formally renounce my fatherhood. I officially recognize the fact that even though you sprang from the fruit of my loins, I have no control over you whatsoever."

"Welcome to the real world," I said, patting him on his arm again. "So what was this news you had?"

"There's much to be said for vasectomies," he muttered as he plopped down in the chair behind his desk.

"You're quickly slipping into the 'ew' zone. The news? For me? That you heard and you're not telling me?"

He sighed heavily, like it was such a big deal to tell me, but finally said, "Do you remember a few weeks ago when I told you about Dr. Morrison's daughter who was going to find herself in Nepal for a month?"

I started jumping up and down even before he finished talking. "I got the job; I got the job!"

"Yes, you got the job. Dr. Morrison spoke to the head

of the zoology department at the Bolte Museum with the upshot that you will be allowed to fill in for Melissa for the month of August."

I did a very cool victory dance around the room. "I got the job; I got the job."

Brother made a pretend frown. "You're not having some sort of attack, are you? All that jerking of your arms and legs. . . . Oh, wait, you're *dancing*."

"Ha-ha." I stopped long enough to whap him on the arm. "So funny I almost laughed up my spleen. I have a job! Coolio!"

One-half of his unibrow rose. "Aren't you even interested in what the job is?"

"Nope. I like animals, so it'll be OK." I started toward the door. "Gotta call Holly and tell her she's not the only one who will be making oodles of money." I paused at the door and looked back. "It does pay great, huge gobs of money, right? 'Cause it's a museum job? I need money, Brother. That allowance you give me is positively minuscule."

"You get a perfectly acceptable allowance—"

"Yeah, it's fine if you don't have a life or anything, but excuse me, I do! I want to go to movies, and buy CDs, and clothes, and makeup, and presents for people, and go to places like London. I'm seventeen, Brother! Money is not just an option when you're seventeen; it's a requirement!"

"You'll find out the pay rate when you go in on Monday," Brother said, his voice tired. I stood there for a minute looking at him. You know, really looking at him. There were black circles under his eyes, and with his hair cut all butch, he looked old. Really old. Older than he was, and we both know he's ancient.

"Are you all right?" I asked, suddenly worried about him.

He looked surprised and rubbed his forehead before answering. "Are you inquiring into my general health or mental state?"

"Brother, we both know your mental state is Froot Loop city," I said, trying to squish down the sick feeling of worry that was boiling up in my stomach. "You don't, like, have cancer or something, and you're not telling me because you don't want to ruin my last month in England—the last and greatest month, because not only is Dru coming to visit for a couple of days, but Fang will be coming home from New Zealand in a week, and I'll finally be able to pin him down about the whole girl/guy thing? You're not hiding the fact that you're going to croak soon, are you?"

"No," he said, rubbing his head again. "It's not that."

"Oh. Good." I waited a few seconds for him to tell me the problem, but he didn't. He just sat there looking old. Part of me wanted to ignore it, but the other part of me, the really annoying part, had me adding, "I wouldn't like it if you were sick."

He stopped rubbing his head and did that old-guy blink a couple of times. "Thank you, Emily. I know how much that admission must have cost you."

"I'd probably even cry."

He cleared his throat in embarrassment and rubbed the bridge of his nose. "Would you, indeed? I'm very touched. I didn't know you cared."

"Not in front of anyone, though," I figured I'd better add. "Because you know how my nose goes all snot-locker when I cry, and my face turns red, and my mascara runs and stuff. But I'd cry where no one could see me."

He sighed one more time. "No, I guess I couldn't expect you to be snot-lockerish in front of people. Good night, Emily."

"Nighty-night," I said, and beetled off to my room feeling all warm and fuzzy. Sometimes you just have to let the ancient ones know they matter, even when they annoy you to death. Did I tell you that I'm not speaking to Mom? She's trying to get me to start packing now, even though we won't be going home to Seattle until the thirtieth of the month. Like I want to spend my last precious month packing stuff? Gah!

Anyhoo, I'll let you know tomorrow how the new job goes. It's bound to be fun working with animals in a museum, don't you think? I thought I was going to have to end up working at the kids' summer camp with Holly, but woo-hoo, I have a museum job!

How's Felix the cat? What did you guys do this weekend? And are you getting excited about coming to England? It's a real pain in the butt that your mom could only afford two weeks in Europe, but oh, well, at least we'll be together for four days! I can't wait for you to meet my friends here. I can't wait for you to drool over Fang.

I sure miss him. It's been like forever since he went off to work on his cousin's farm.

Tell all about what you're packing!

Hugs and smooches.
~Em

Subject: re: Hippo birdies 2 ewe!
From: Emmers@britsahoy.co.uk
To: fbaxter@ganglia.co.nz
Date: 1 August 2004 10:40 pm

Fang wrote:
> *Thank you for the birthday card and wishes. I spent*
> *the day helping my cousin repairing a fence that had*
> *been destroyed by cattle from the neighboring farm,*
> *but I appreciated the card and the CD you made for*
> *me. I'll be home on the eighth, so stop worrying.*

You had to work on your birthday? Sheesh! Oh well, I suppose that's how they do things there. I'm so happy you'll be home soon! I can't wait to hear all about your summer in NZ . . . no, wait, you said it was winter there, huh? Whatever, I can't wait to hear about it.

I ran into Aidan the other day. He's just as icky as ever, although he didn't go all potty-mouth on me like he has in the past. And he asked where you were, which I thought was nice, and he said he is going to Oxford in the fall, so I guess everything worked out with him transferring schools. He didn't ask about Devon, though. Guess he's still mad about Devon beating him up after we got back from Paris. I know you and Dev had kind of given Aidan up, so hopefully you won't be too hurt or anything that he's still a poophead.

There's loads more I have to tell you. It's been really strange with you gone. I wish you had come back in July, like you were going to, but I'm not going to yell at you about that. Aren't you impressed? I've been doing some thinking, Fang, and . . . um . . . never mind. I'll tell you when you get home.

I'm really, *really* glad you're coming back.

Emily

Subject: Want some cheese with that whine?
From: Emmers@britsahoy.co.uk
To: Devonator@skynetcomm.com
Date: 1 August 2004 10:53 pm

Devonator wrote:
> *so I won't be back to England for a couple more weeks.*
> *I've got the villa to myself, which is cool, but it would*
> *be more fun with you here. Any way you can come*
> *out for a few days? My uncle won't be back from Rome*
> *for a few weeks, so it's cool if you can come. You can*
> *even bring Holly, if her parents will let her go to*
> *Greece.*

Man, I'd love to come to Greece, but I just can't. I've got a job starting tomorrow—score! A real job, too, one in a museum and everything! So I can't come, but thank you for asking. I miss you like mad! You may think it's no fun not knowing anyone in Greece, but I know you, Dev—you're a babe magnet. I bet you have girls crawling all over you.

I, on the other hand, am here by my sad and lonesome self. Fang is gone, you are gone, Holly spends most of her weekends going up to Scotland to see Ruaraidh, even Bess has been busy, what with her witch training and stuff. My mom is obsessed with packing, and Brother is downright weird.

Anyway, I can't wait for you to come home. You'll be back before I have to go, right? You're my best guy friend, Dev, even if you're not my boyfriend anymore. Any guy who lets me barf on him (twice!) and still wants to hang with me is pretty fabu. I just couldn't leave England without seeing you again.

Hugsies!
Emily

They Wear WHAT Under Their Kilts?

by Katie Maxwell

Subject: Emily's Glossary for People Who Haven't Been to Scotland
From: Mrs.Legolas@kiltnet.com
To: Dru@seattlegrrl.com

Faffing about: running around doing nothing. In other words, spending a month supposedly doing work experience on a Scottish sheep farm, but really spending days on Kilt Watch at the nearest castle.

Schottie: Scottish Hottie, also known as Ruaraidh.

Mad schnoogles: the British way of saying big smoochy kisses. Will admit it sounds v. smart to say it that way.

Bunch of yobbos: a group of mindless idiots. In Scotland, can also mean sheep.

Stooshie: uproar, as in, "If Holly thinks she can take Ruaraidh from me without causing a stooshie, she's out of her mind!"

Sheep dip: not an appetizer.

Didn't want this book to end?

There's more waiting at **www.smoochya.com**:

Win FREE books and makeup!
Read excerpts from other books!
Chat with the authors!
Horoscopes!
Quizzes!